"That was just one night," she said huskily.

"Marriage is for—for—" She swallowed down the word as if she suddenly feared expressing it. "Marriage is different."

"Not that different."

Slowly he lifted her, drawing her out of her seat and pulling her up the length of his body. The rich blue silk of her dress whispered against him and her perfume reached out to enclose him. Had she worn this to give herself some much-needed courage to face yet another suitor?

"You know what that one night was like..." His voice was low and husky, rough-edged and raw. "Imagine a lifetime of such nights—each one better than the last."

He saw her throat move as she swallowed hard, the way a pink tongue snaked out to moisten her dry lips.

"Marriage is more than just nights."

"But these won't be just nights. They will be amazing, spectacular nights. Nights you will never forget. Nights you will spend your days longing for, your sleep dreaming of."

Harlequin Presents®

The
Alcolar Family

*Proud, modern-day Spanish aristocrats—
passion is their birthright!*

Harlequin Presents® is proud to present
international bestselling author Kate Walker's new
ALCOLAR FAMILY miniseries.

Meet the Alcolar Family:

Joaquin: The firstborn and only legitimate Alcolar
son. Can he forget his no-commitment rule and
make his twelve-month mistress his wife?

Alex: He may be half-English, but he's all Alcolar.
A long-ago lover has claimed he's her husband—
now he'll claim his wife!

Alex's story, Wife for Real, *is a free online read
at www.eHarlequin.com*

Ramón: The beloved illegitimate son, he gets
more than he bargained for in his carefully
planned marriage of convenience!

Mercedes: Can the only Alcolar daughter
find the man who is her match?

Find out in *Bound by Blackmail* #2504
Coming in November 2005

Kate Walker is the author of more than
40 romance novels for Harlequin Presents®.
To find out about Kate, and her forthcoming
books, visit her Web site at www.kate-walker.com

Kate Walker

THE SPANIARD'S INCONVENIENT WIFE

The Alcolar Family

HARLEQUIN®

TORONTO • NEW YORK • LONDON
AMSTERDAM • PARIS • SYDNEY • HAMBURG
STOCKHOLM • ATHENS • TOKYO • MILAN • MADRID
PRAGUE • WARSAW • BUDAPEST • AUCKLAND

For Barbara, who knows more
about Ramón than most.

And of course, for Peter, too.
Thank you for your friendship.

ISBN 0-373-12498-8

THE SPANIARD'S INCONVENIENT WIFE

First North American Publication 2005.

Copyright © 2005 by Kate Walker.

CHAPTER ONE

ESTRELLA stood with her fingers on the handle of the door, fighting for calm. She needed to prepare herself for the confrontation that was ahead of her. For the meeting with the man who was waiting for her on the far side of that door.

She'd thought all this was over; that her father had given up on the idea of marrying her off to the nearest available candidate. But just now he had marched into her room, barely troubling to slam his hand against the wood in a pretence of a knock, and told her that the man with whom he had had such an important business meeting that afternoon wanted to see her, right now. And she had known, with a desperate, sinking feeling in the pit of her stomach, that she had been wrong, and it was starting again.

If she could have run away, she would have done. If she could have gone somewhere and hidden, concealing herself until this man lost patience and left in a rage, then she would have taken that path. But experience had shown her that face-to-face confrontation was the only way to handle this.

So she dragged in another jagged breath, smoothed a slightly unsteady hand over the black sleekness of her hair, straightened her narrow shoulders, forced herself to turn the handle, and went in.

He was standing by the big window at the far end of the room. Big and strong, and darkly silhouetted against the light, his face turned away from her, looking out at the garden below.

'You are Señor Dario? Señor Ramón Juan Francisco Dario?'

The tension in her body touched her voice as well, making it cold and tight and totally unwelcoming, bringing his head round with a jerk.

'I am. And you are Estrella Medrano?' His response was as stiff and unwelcoming as her voice had been.

'My father said that you wanted to see me.'

She didn't trouble to answer the question, and his brows drew sharply together in disapproval or anger at the abruptness of her opening, the coldness of her tone.

But what had he expected? That she would spend time on polite courtesies? Knowing why he was here, she certainly didn't intend to chat with him.

'I wanted to talk to you, yes.'

'But I understood that you came here to see my father?'

'Yes—I wanted to buy the TV company.'

'And did you succeed?'

'We're—still negotiating.'

Of course, Estrella reflected cynically. Of course they were still negotiating. The deal would not be signed until this man fulfilled her father's demands. If she had had any lingering doubts, they vanished now. 'Still negotiating' meant only one thing. He was another one. Another in the long line of would-be husbands that her father thought he had bought for her.

'Too expensive for you?' she enquired carefully, stroking uncomfortably damp palms down the side of the narrow black skirt she wore with a tailored white blouse.

'No, not at all. I would pay almost any price.'

He was coming towards her as he spoke and that lithe, loose-limbed lope seemed full of a potent energy, an energy that had to be held back, reined in, so as to be controlled enough to stay indoors. Just watching him move she felt the tiny hairs on the back of her neck rise in instinctive response, but whether of fear or hostility she had no way of knowing. She only knew that, large as it was, this elegant sitting room suddenly seemed too small, too confining for the elemental force of his power.

'So you want the company very much?'

'Yes. Yes, I do.'

He must do if he was prepared to go along with her father's plan like this. If he was prepared to sell himself—and buy her—in order to acquire what he wanted. Her father must have seen that in him and decided he had got just the right man this time.

If she had any sense, then now was the moment when she should tell him that she knew exactly what was going on and that there was no point in taking things any further. That, no matter what her father had led him to believe, there was no way she wanted to hear his proposal. Certainly no way she was ever going to accept it.

But she didn't. And, to tell the truth, she had no idea exactly why she didn't.

He was not at all what she had expected, this Ramón Dario. For one thing, she had thought that he would be like his father. Reuben Dario had been a big, dark bull of a man, heavy and thickset, with ebony hair and equally black eyes. And no one, not even his mother, could have called him handsome.

But this man was stunning. And in so many ways he was almost the opposite of his father, reversing rather than matching Dario senior's looks and colouring.

He was much taller, for one thing, and although his hair was dark it was shot through with flashes of copper that made it gleam in the afternoon sunlight slanting through the windows so that the overall effect was one of burnished bronze rather than polished ebony. His eyes, in contrast, were cool, the clear, watchful grey of a storm-washed sky after a torrential downpour, and they were set in a harshly carved face that seemed all planes and angles, the smooth skin tanned rather than swarthy like his father's.

But then of course she was forgetting that Ramón Dario was only half Spanish. His mother, who had died years ago, when this man was just a baby, had been an Englishwoman.

The extra inches of height went with a much less solid build so that if he had been put next to Reuben—or indeed her own father—he would have looked almost slender. But it was obvious that his less bulky frame was taut with whip-cord-strong muscle, the broad shoulders under the perfectly tailored jacket strong and straight, the long legs planted firmly on the rich red carpeting.

'So why would you want to see me?' she managed. As if she didn't know.

'I wanted to talk to you.'

'And what you want—you get?'

He didn't like her attitude; that much was obvious. The frown that had marked his face wasn't easing; if anything it was growing darker, more dangerous. But she was beyond caring.

She wanted this over and done with so that she could get away again. Back to her room. Back to the isolation she had grown so accustomed to. Back to her father's black glares and lectures and furious disapproval, the disapproval she'd lived with so long that it was as if she had never, ever seen any other expression on his face. Back to local society's censure and the whispering behind their hands, the way that conversations suddenly died when she walked into a room.

'That's the one…' people said. 'That's the Medrano girl; the one who enticed Carlos Perea away from his wife. Leaving her with two small children to care for all on her own. And him old enough to be the little hussy's father…'

'Won't you sit down?'

He indicated a chair with a wave of his hand.

'Will I need to?'

There was no reason at all why her heart should pulse high up in her throat at the thought of even moving closer to him. Why her senses should be so painfully alert to this man's physical presence. Even the faint tang of his cologne, reaching her on the air as he moved, made her nerves tug, her nostrils flare as if to inhale more of the spicy scent. Heat flooded her veins, making her shift uneasily where she stood.

She had never been this close to any of the others. Never been this close to any man if it came to that. Not since Carlos.

'I'd rather stand.'

'I thought you would prefer to be comfortable.'

'To tell you the truth, I'd prefer to be anywhere but here.'

'I can assure you I won't keep you long.'

His tone was stiff and cold, the words bitten off sharply. The thought that he actually felt he could show disapproval of her sparked the temper she had been struggling to keep under control.

'And I can assure you that I have no interest in anything you want to say to me.'

She'd really got to him now. It was obvious from the way that his breath hissed between his teeth, the icy glare that flashed in her direction.

'Might I suggest you wait till I've actually said something?'

He had been eyeing her up from the moment she had walked into the room, but now that steely grey gaze raked over every inch of her from her head to her toes, the cold-eyed look making her feel as if she were a prize piece of breeding stock that didn't quite come up to expectations.

None of the others had ever made her feel quite as bad as this. Her fingers twitched with the need to wipe that look from his face, and her tongue itched to tell him exactly what she thought. But the self-control she had grown so used to imposing on herself held her back.

'Then say it,' was all she could manage.

'All right, I will.'

One strong hand raked through the gleaming dark hair, ruffling it wildly for a moment before it fell back into place with the ease and discipline of what was obviously a highly skilled and probably very expensive cut. Suddenly, in spite of herself, Estrella found herself regretting the speed with which that control and order were restored. Because just for a moment, in those few fleeting seconds, she had seen almost another Ramón Dario. A man very far removed from the guarded, distant person he had been almost ever since she had come into the room.

He would look like that in bed, she found herself thinking, a deep honeyed beat of sensuality starting low down in her body. With his hair ruffled and those heavy-lidded grey eyes still softened with sleep, only half open, gleaming, smiling up into the face of the woman...

She was shocked to find that the image made her heart pick up a beat, then jump into double-quick time. She had never felt like this in her life before. Never. Not even with Carlos.

Carlos who had been the start of all this. Whose malign influence could still reach out and touch her life, even after all this time. Even from the grave.

But Carlos had never been able to make her feel like this.

What was she thinking of? She couldn't help it. Something in this man tugged at everything that was female in her.

'There is a problem—*we* have a problem.'

Ramón Dario's voice brought her crashing back to the

bitterness of reality, wiping away the wanton fantasies at a single blow.

'What do you mean, we? Why do you link the two of us together in that way?'

'Because your father linked us together.'

So now they were coming to it. Suddenly, when every other time before she had just wanted this moment over and done with, out of the way as quickly as possible, to her total shock she found that she felt exactly the opposite. She wished she could reach out now—put a hand to his mouth and stop him. Stop him from making the proposal that her father and some promise of riches had enticed from him.

Because if he did propose, then she would have to give him an answer.

And the answer would have to be no.

It was always no. Ever since her father had decided to 'redeem' her from the shadow of her past, by procuring, there really was no other word for it, a respectable and hope-fully financially secure marriage, she had had to endure this situation over and over. If Ramón Dario thought he could acquire her as part of a business deal, as an extra that came along with his precious television company, then he was going to get the same answer as the rest.

No.

But even as the thought crossed her mind and determination firmed her spine, she knew a tiny, unwanted quiver of regret. For the first time ever, since her father had started this appalling campaign to get her married, she was actually wondering...

'Your father suggested a price I could happily accept,' Ramón continued, clearly taking her silence for encourage ment. 'And I want the company! But there are conditions. These conditions affect you. Your father wants me to marry you. He won't sell me the company unless I do.'

It was only what she had been expecting, but all the same Estrella knew a terrible sense of loss at the realisation that now there was no going back. There was no hope that maybe, just this once, this man might have been the one who couldn't be bought.

That tiny, stupid little hope had crept in from nowhere. It had been born because this Ramón Dario wasn't taking things in the way she'd been anticipating. In fact, he wasn't dealing with the situation as anyone else had ever done. And as a result she had had no idea how to handle him.

But now it seemed that he was just like all the others after all. Ruthless, greedy, determined to get what he wanted, no matter who or what stood in his way. And totally careless of her feelings in the matter.

'Estrella,' Ramón said when despair and disappointment held her silent. 'Did you hear what I said? Your father wants me to marry you.'

'I know,' she said softly; so softly that at first he didn't quite hear her. But then a moment later the words registered.

'You know!' Ramón echoed, unable to believe what he had heard.

How could she be so calm about it? So indifferent to what her father had been after? Or was it—his guts twisted sharply on a wave of disgust—was it that she had been involved from the start? That she had been a party to the whole thing; perhaps had even selected him and told her father that he was her choice? The thought made him feel like a piece of meat on a shop counter. It curdled in his stomach, and angry revulsion thickened his voice when he turned on her again.

'Am I hearing right? Did you say you know?'

'Yes.'

It was lower even than before, but this time he was waiting for it, watching the movement of her lips intently, so that he saw as much as heard the word leave her mouth.

'What—how did you know? How did you know?' he repeated more emphatically when she didn't answer. 'I think I have the right to an explanation, seeing as you've been playing with my life.'

That got to her. Her chin came up defiantly, ebony eyes flashing.

'Okay—you can have your explanation, but I warn you, you won't like it. Do you think you're the first? Do you think you're the only man my father has tried to buy for me?'

'I'm not?'

She shook her head violently so that the black hair flew wildly around her suddenly colourless face.

'You're not even the second—or the third.'

Was she determined to crush his ego completely—to list every single man who had been chosen before him? Every man she would have preferred.

'Spare me the gory details,' he grated. 'Just give me a round number.'

This was the Estrella Medrano that Ramón had been led to expect; the woman he had heard that she was. He'd let himself be distracted by the way that she looked, because she hadn't been at all as he had expected. She wasn't even close to the way he had imagined her. His first sight of her had surprised him so much that he had found himself staring blankly at her when she had appeared in the doorway

In the picture he had formed of her in his mind, she had been small, and voluptuous, and definitely a little wild. The woman who had a reputation like Estrella Medrano would have to be wild. He had expected short hair and even shorter skirts, and cosmetics applied with a heavy hand. He had expected colour and clash in her clothing, and of course that defiance that her story had led him to be sure he would see.

Instead she was taller, slimmer, quieter—altogether sleeker and more elegant than he had ever imagined. From her oval-shaped face with its high, slanting cheekbones to the slim, fine boned feet in the simple black pumps, she was restraint personified. Only the fall of her rich silky hair, black and shining as polished jet, hinted at an uncontrolled element in her that didn't quite fit with the plain white blouse and simple, beautifully cut skirt, severe as a nun's habit.

She was beautiful. She was stunning, and sexy as hell—but as cold and hard as a brilliant diamond.

If he hadn't believed the tales of her past before, he believed them now. Oh, yes, he believed them! He'd just about had confirmation from her own mouth—not of the past perhaps—but of the calculating way she and her father had got together to select their prey, hunt it down, try to capture it.

'How many?'

'Ten.' It was cold and clear and hard as stone. 'Before you there were nine others. You're the tenth.'

Her head inclined slightly at the sound of his vicious, savage-toned curse, but other than that she showed no sign of reaction.

'I warned you you wouldn't like it.'

'You're damn right I don't like it,' Ramón growled. 'I don't like it and I don't like you. I don't like being manipulated.'

'I didn't manipulate...' she began, but then her voice trailed off as her wide dark eyes met the anger that he knew must be showing in his face.

'You knew what was going on.'

'I—yes,' she admitted.

'And you didn't think it might be—courteous at the very least to let me know that you knew?'

But that had her lifting her chin again, bringing those dark eyes up to lock with his as if daring him to go on with this line of questioning.

'You're a fine one to talk about courtesy!' she flung at him. 'Or about what I should or should not have said to you! After all, you're the one who was prepared to go along with my father's plan!'

But Ramón was not having that. He had known so clearly what he meant to do from the moment that Alfredo Medrano had made his appalling suggestion. No, it hadn't been a suggestion, more a command issued from the height of the autocratic older man's belief in his own superiority. A decree of what he wanted—and he expected that everyone would jump to give him what he demanded.

And because Ramón had known what he expected, he fully intended to thwart him totally.

'Hell, no!' he cut in savagely.

'No?' Estrella questioned ironically, one fine black brow lifting in mocking enquiry. 'Then what are you doing here?'

It was a question he was forced to ask himself. What the devil was he doing here, being subjected to a scolding by this dark-eyed harridan?

This beautiful, dark-eyed harridan.

This beautiful, sexy, dark-eyed, full-lipped harridan.

This sexy, dark-eyed harridan whose angry stance had pulled her spine so straight, setting her hands so firmly on her slender hips, that the sensual enticement of her full breasts was thrust forward, impossible to ignore. And whose furious temper had put rich flags of colour on the golden skin of her face, high up on the elegant, slanting cheekbones.

How could she do this? How did she do it? How could

she be so aggressive, so cynical, so hostile, so damn infuriating—and still look so beautiful and appealing that he just couldn't get his mind to work straight?

'You know only too well why I'm here—I came to—'

'You originally came to negotiate the sale of the company, I know that! But you admitted that my father wouldn't sell.'

'Unless I agreed to his conditions.'

'Unless you agreed to his conditions,' Estrella echoed mockingly. 'And then you stayed. I wonder why.'

'You know why I stayed,' he growled, struggling to keep his thoughts from wandering, fighting against the kick of carnal need that almost had him doubling up in pain. His mouth had dried so suddenly that it made his voice rough and harsh, rasping as if from a sore and inflamed throat. 'I stayed to talk to you.'

'To follow my father's orders and get me to marry you!'

The words came out on a rush of air as she whirled away from him, circling the big leather armchair until she was behind it, the wide, high back acting as a barrier between them and a defensive shield as she faced him once again.

'You can think that if you want.'

'You told me how much you wanted the TV company.'

With the provocation of her body hidden behind the big chair, it should have been easier to think more clearly, but that couldn't be further from the truth. The fact was that all he could think about was the swift, brief glimpse he had had of her taut, rounded behind in the sexily tight black skirt as she'd swung away from him, the sway of her hips as she'd moved. He felt hard and hot and hungry and thinking clearly was the last thing he was capable of doing.

'Oh, I wanted it—but not that badly! Not badly enough to want to tie myself to you!'

He'd caught her on the raw there, he noted with grim

satisfaction. She'd actually flinched, the slim, elegantly manicured fingers resting on the back of the chair tightening convulsively, digging into the burgundy leather. The satisfaction of seeing her react with something more than scorn pulled at his darkest feelings and a terrible imp of malice urged him to score another hit while he could.

'I've no thought of marrying any time soon. Why should I want to tie myself down when there are hundreds of beautiful women all over Catalonia and beyond? And even if I was, I do have some pride. I would much prefer to choose my own bride than marry someone I had to be bribed to wed.'

'Well don't worry—you won't even get the chance!'

He didn't mince his words, did he? Estrella fought a sharp little battle with herself to hide the sting of his barbed attack, refusing to let the tears threaten, even though they pricked hard at the backs of her eyes. She'd wept enough in the past over men who weren't worth it—one man in particular. And after being emotionally savaged by an expert like Carlos, petty insults like this were a piece of cake.

Or at least they should have been. But somehow this man's knife thrusts got under her skin, scoring brutal wounds along her soul.

'I wouldn't marry you if my life and the future of mankind depended on it!' she flung at him. 'If you were to ask me—'

'Which I won't.'

'If you were to ask me,' Estrella persisted through gritted teeth, 'I'd throw the words right back in your face and love every second of it.'

'Well, enjoy the feeling of imagining it,' Ramón tossed back. 'Because, believe me, that's as close as you'll ever get to doing it. I've no intention of putting my head in a noose just so that you can pull it tight around my throat, even if you are the sexiest thing on two legs I've seen in a long, long time.'

CHAPTER TWO

THE sexiest thing on two legs...

Estrella couldn't believe what she was hearing. Had Ramón really said—?

A warm, intoxicating sense of pleasure flooded her veins, making her head swim with sudden and purely feminine delight. In spite of herself she couldn't stop a swift, tiny smile from tugging at the corners of her lips. It was brief as a heartbeat; there and gone in a second. But he caught it and his black brows twitched together in an even harsher frown.

'Oh, you liked that did you,' he drawled cynically. 'You liked the thought that I find you sexy? Well, don't think that you can use it to your advantage. I'm not so desperate that I would want Carlos Perea's cast-offs—even if they do come with a substantial bribe of the TV company in the form of a dowry. I'd want much more than that.'

'Well, you could have had more.'

This time Estrella's brief, tight smile had none of the fleeting warmth and delight of just moments before.

'If you'd played your cards right, my father would have settled anything on you. Everything you wanted—right down to the castle and the title that goes with it. If you'd given him a grandson, his gratitude would have known no bounds.'

The look that crossed his stunning face puzzled her. As did the momentary pause before he came back at her. She'd said something that had hit home to him—but what? She barely had time to formulate the question before his ex-

pression changed again, the cold-eyed sneer coming back
with a vengeance.

'Thanks, but no, thanks,' he drawled. 'Even with the
added incentives the deal is still way too expensive.'

'I wasn't offering,' Estrella snapped back. 'I was simply
pointing out just what you've missed. There is no deal on
offer, Señor Dario, nor ever will be—at least not where
you're concerned.'

Coming out from behind the chair, she marched across
the room towards the door, twisting the handle with a violence that made her wish it were his neck, and smiled grimly
to herself at the thought.

'All negotiations are closed,' she said, opening the door
wide and standing aside so as to give him more than enough
space to get through without having to come within an inch
of her. 'This meeting is at an end. I would appreciate it if
you would leave.'

'Willingly,' Ramón returned, sharp as a stiletto blade, and
he actually sketched a small, cynical parody of a courtly
bow in her direction before he moved too.

His every stride, the tautly upright, uptight way he held
his strong body, told exactly the mood he was in. He was
furious, and it showed. He also despised her totally, wished
he were anywhere but here, and couldn't get out of the room
quickly enough.

Which made a total nonsense of the sudden, overwhelming feeling she had: the impossible, unbelievable, but savage
sense of regret that tore at her with the realisation that in
two minutes, maybe less, he would be gone. And she would
never see him again.

But that was what she wanted, wasn't it? To have him
out of her life, never to see him again. Never to have to
look into his eyes and see the burning scorn, the icy contempt that made her shiver like a leaf in the wind.

It was what she wanted, but, just watching him, she was a prey to a sudden shaft of pure need. She didn't know how, she didn't know why, but something about this man had hit home to all that was female in her. She had been able to let all the others go without a single qualm—but not him. He hadn't even touched her—or kissed her and if she let him go now, like this, then he never would.

The need to have known this man's kiss, if only once in her lifetime, was so overpowering that she almost spoke of it. She actually opened her mouth to beg him to stay, just for a moment. To pause and turn away from his determined path.

But she didn't dare. Her tongue seemed tied into knots and she could only watch in silence as Ramón continued on his way towards the open door.

But not out of the door.

Instead, just as he came near, he made a tiny detour, coming close to her instead. The look in his eyes warned her, but before Estrella could quite work out just what was in his mind he had already acted.

Reaching out, he caught hold of her shoulders, pulling her up to him with a sudden, jerky movement. All the breath escaped from her lungs in a gasp as her breasts made contact with the hard, warm wall of his chest, and she had no time to think, or resist, before his hand came under her chin and pushed it upwards so that her angry black eyes clashed with the cool, assessing grey of his.

'I'll leave,' he muttered roughly, his voice thick with suppressed rage and something else, something that made her shiver inwardly, but whether in fear or a thread of excited anticipation, she was unable to say. 'I'll leave—and willingly—but first there's something I just have to do.'

Storm cloud eyes dropped to her lips just in time to catch

her slicking them nervously with her tongue before his gaze flicked back up to meet her nervous ebony one.

'Something I've been wanting to do since the moment I met you. Something you've been tempting me to do since you walked through that door.'

'I—' Estrella tried to protest, but the words were crushed back down her throat as his mouth came down on hers, taking possession of her lips with a wildly demanding hunger that struck with all the force of a tidal wave.

A tidal wave that swept her away completely with its power, driving all thoughts from her mind. Instead, she was only aware of sensation, of the throbbing pulse of the blood at her temples, the heat of her skin, the way that the world seemed to swirl around her.

And of Ramón.

Ramón, so big and dark and strong, his arms enclosing her, his lips on hers, his skin against her skin, his breath on her face. The scent of him was in her nostrils, clean and subtly musky, and the warmth of his body was all around her, pervading every nerve, every cell until she was unable to tell which was Ramón, and which was her.

Unable to stop herself, she kissed him right back. Her mouth opened under his, her lips not forced apart but responding, enticing, welcoming the sensual slide and caress of his tongue, meeting its silky exploration with her own.

Her hands fluttered up to the width of his shoulders under the finely tailored jacket. They touched, explored, lingered for a moment, but then, unsatisfied, they moved again, upwards, to slide over his neck, then combing her fingers through the silky darkness of his hair.

'Ramón...'

It was just a murmur against his mouth, his name choked out with no control, no coherent thought.

'Ramón...' she sighed again and felt his soft, faintly

shaken laughter against her cheek before he drew her close again and took her mouth once more.

Driven by the wild heat uncoiling in the pit of her stomach and spreading lower, pooling between her legs, she couldn't stop herself from crushing up against him, fitting her pelvis to his and feeling the swollen evidence of a hungry desire for more than just a kiss.

The rough, incoherent sound he made in his throat in response worked on her already heated senses like the most ardent encouragement, so that the fingers in his hair twisted and tangled in the dark strands, clutching tightly as she tugged his head down even more, pressing her mouth closer to his.

The heat of his palms was on her ribcage, burning through the fine cotton of her shirt, and he was walking her backwards, clumsily, awkwardly, urgently backwards until they came up hard against the wall. With the wall at her back and the fierce, hot pressure that was all Ramón crushed up against her front, Estrella should have felt trapped, but instead the sensation that burned through her was exactly the opposite.

She wanted more. More of this heat, this power. More of the hectic pulse that was sending her heart rate skyrocketing. More of the heavier, harder throb that centred at the joining of her thighs, making her shift restlessly at its urging. More of the wild and heady sensations that were making her head swim.

She wanted more of Ramón's kisses, more of his touch. She wanted his hands to move upwards, higher—higher. Her breasts ached with the need to feel his hard fingers against them, caressing, teasing… And the erotic hunger was so strong that she actually moaned aloud in her need.

The next moment, to her horror, it was as if the sound had been a slap in the face to Ramón. Or a shout of warning, telling him that this could not go on. Because he suddenly stilled, paused, then lifted his head with deliberate slowness, looking deep into her eyes as he did so.

And as that cold, steely gaze burned into hers she felt the jarring shock of the unwanted return to reality, the abrupt descent from the giddy heights of passion to this cold, hard moment making her feel faintly nauseous. Desperately struggling with a numb sense of shock at her own behaviour, and the knowledge that the way Ramón was looking at her was a million miles away from lover-like, she tried to school her features into a mask of cold indifference but had no idea at all whether she had even come close to succeeding.

'*Madre de Dios…*' Ramón breathed rawly. '*Madre de Dios.*'

She looked as dazed as he felt, Ramón acknowledged through the haze of unfocused thoughts, sexual imaginings and yearning demand that filled what might laughingly have been called his brain. He was dazed and knocked sideways by the wild and uncontrollable passion that had suddenly flared between them.

Suddenly but not unexpectedly. It had been what he had wanted almost from the moment he had met her. All he had wanted and more.

He had wanted her. Hadn't been able to resist the urge to kiss her. Hadn't been able to hold back when the chance had come to take her into his arms and kiss the haughty condescension from her face.

What he hadn't anticipated had been her response. He had thought that kissing her would have been like kissing a brick wall, cold and hard and totally unyielding.

Instead she had been pure fire in his arms. She had ignited like a firework, becoming nothing but heat and flame, flashing lightning, whirling sparks that had exploded inside his head. In that moment his control had gone into total meltdown. He hadn't known where he was or who he was, had had no idea what was happening. His whole being had been concentrated on one desire: the need to know this woman as intimately and as totally as he could. His senses screamed to have her, his body harder and hotter than it had ever been before in his life. Another moment more and he would have ripped her clothes from her and flung her down onto the floor, easing the ravenous demand of his hungry body in her responsive and willing flesh.

It was only when that small, moaning cry had brought him to a sudden awareness of where he was and who she was that any sense of reality had returned. With that real- isation had come a rush of sanity that had felt like a brutal blow to the side of his head, forcing him to tear his mouth away from hers and fight desperately for control over the excruciating burn of frustration low down in his groin.

'Well, how about that?' he forced himself to drawl, as if he weren't in the least affected by the sudden tidal wave of passion that had broken over him. Only by blanking off his mind from the rest of his still hungry body could he keep his voice under control, stop the words from breaking harshly in the middle.

'"All negotiations are closed,"' he quoted, echoing her words of what seemed like a lifetime ago but had in fact only been a couple of heated, mind-blowing minutes. '"This meeting is at an end." Oh, my dear Doña Estrella—is that how you dismiss all your business partners? With a kiss?'

'I—'

Estrella opened her mouth to answer him, then clearly lost control of her voice and had to close it again, swallow- ing hard and hurriedly.

'I didn't kiss you,' she managed at last. 'As I remember it, you were the one who kissed me. And we are not partners, not by any stretch of the imagination. Not business partners or—or any other kind of partners at all.'

'Of course not,' Ramón accompanied the words with a cynical smile. 'But as I remember it, you were definitely not holding back. Quite the opposite, in fact.'

Holding her huge, dazed eyes with his, he let his smile grow as he remembered.

'"I wouldn't marry you if my life and the future of mankind depended on it,"' he quoted again, watching her sharp, embarrassed start of response as she recognised her own words. 'Not marry me, perhaps, Doña Medrano, but I'd be willing to bet that if I'd asked you to come to bed with me then, you'd have been there like a shot. You probably still would.'

She drew in a brusque little breath and opened her mouth to rage at him in protest. But Ramón broke in again swiftly, before she even had time to speak a word.

'But, much as I would like to take you up on what you're offering, I'm afraid I'm going to have to decline. If there was one thing that kiss taught me then it's that I was right the first time—any deal with you is going to cost way too much. And frankly, I don't think you're worth it.'

He was just going to have to pray that she bought that, he told himself as he turned and walked away. He was not going to look back; not going to give her a chance to argue with him or say anything more. Because the truth was that he really didn't think he had any chance of convincing her if he spoke again.

Hell, he hadn't even convinced himself.

If she had said one word of encouragement to him—if even now she called to him, asked him to come back, he knew damn well that he would do it. He couldn't not do it. He wanted her so much that even walking was agony, with his body still totally aroused and heatedly demanding the satisfaction he had refused to give it.

If he stopped, if he paused, he would turn. If he turned, he would see her—and she would see him. She couldn't be unaware of the physical state he was in, not unless she was blind and stupid, and he knew she was neither of those. And if he saw her face again, her mouth swollen and pink from his kisses, her black hair mussed and tousled around her face, he wouldn't be able to stop himself from going back to her, gathering her up into his arms, and continuing from where they had left off—and this time nothing, but nothing, would stop him from taking what he wanted. Even if Alfredo himself came into the room in the middle of the whole thing.

So he kept on walking. Just putting one foot in front of the other, making himself take his time, not rushing, just strolling—apparently easily. One foot in front of another. He didn't even trouble to make the effort to shut the door, managing to resist the temptation to slam it closed behind him, and cut himself off from Doña Medrano's watchful dark chocolate eyes as she watched him go. And all the way down the long, thickly carpeted corridor he felt the burn of her gaze on him, following him, searing into the strong, taut line of his back, watching and waiting until he came to the staircase at the far end.

Then, just as he turned to go down those stairs he finally heard her voice. Heard her shout after him, her voice floating down the corridor to him.

'Not if my life depended on it, Señor Dario! That's what I said and that's what I meant. And it's certainly going to take a whole lot more than just one kiss to make me change my mind.'

'Then at least we both agree on something.'

Oh, who was she trying to kid? Estrella asked herself,

watching as Ramón waved a careless hand in her direction before marching down the stairs and out of sight. If he had looked back just for a second he would have known her words for the lie they were. He would have seen the way that her eyes followed him, the magnetic effect that every movement, every tilt of his head, every stretch of a muscle had on her so that she could not drag her gaze away. She was sure that he would have seen the dryness of her lips, the hectic flags of colour in her cheeks that were the result of her wildly accelerated heartbeat, and known them as the signs of her uncontrollable response to his ardent kisses.

He had been so right. Appallingly, shockingly, devastatingly right.

'Not if my life and the whole of the future of mankind depended on it.' Miserably she repeated the wild, overblown claim that she had flung after him in an unthinking fury of emotion as she watched him walk away, shaking her head in despair at her own weakness, her own stupidity.

Nothing could have been further from the truth.

She had been his, ripe, ready and available. All he would have had to do was to press his claim a little more, kiss her a little longer, touch her, caress her where she had so ached to be touched, and she would have been his without a moment's hesitation, right here on the floor if that was what he had asked of her.

She still would be, she realised on a shivering blend of fear and tingling delight. If he came back. If she heard his footsteps ascending the staircase again instead of heading downwards. If he appeared at the end of the corridor now and opened his arms she would fly into them, like a bird heading home to its nest. And she would be totally at his mercy, willing to do whatever he asked, however he asked.

She had barely found the strength to resist him this time. She very much doubted that she could ever manage it again.

'Oh, damn you, Ramón Dario!'

The words exploded from her in a fury of emotion, but whether that emotion was anger, or loss, or just the plain bitterness of physical frustration, even she couldn't tell. So instead she gave in to childish petulance, reaching out and slamming the door shut with as much force as she could muster, glorying in the way that the violent sound echoed and reverberated round the room.

'Damn, damn, damn, damn, damn you!'

Just what was happening to her? How could things be like this so hard, so fast?

She had thought that she loved Carlos Perea, but she had insisted on waiting...

But she wasn't in love with this man. How could she be? She had only known Ramón Dario for— A swift glance at the big clock on the wall told her that it was not even half an hour since she had walked into the room. Not even thirty minutes since her father had sent her here to meet the latest of the prospective husbands he believed his money had bought for her.

But with Ramón Dario time hadn't meant anything. She had felt the kick of response deep inside in the first moment she had looked at him. It was as if she had known her destiny. As if her body had recognised a master, the other piece of the jigsaw, someone she was programmed to respond to no matter what.

She was only fooling herself if she thought that, if Ramón called to her, she would be able to resist. She hadn't a hope of holding back from him, no matter how she tried. She might just as well admit that to herself and face the facts, once and for all.

The one, the only good thing about this situation was the fact that, after the way that they had parted, the way that Ramón had stalked to the door and down the corridor away from her, not even sparing her a single glance back, there was no chance that they would ever meet again. If they never met again, then she would never have to struggle with temptation in a fight that she knew she was bound to lose.

If she never saw Ramón Dario again, then she was safe. Safe from him and from herself.

That thought was supposed to comfort her. It should have comforted her.

But in fact it had exactly the opposite effect.

CHAPTER THREE

RAMÓN kicked the door to behind him, tossed his keys onto the nearby dresser and rubbed his hands tiredly over his face before surveying his empty, silent apartment with a grim expression on his dark features.

Something had happened in the past couple of weeks. He wasn't at all sure just what it was or how to explain this new set of feelings he was plagued with. He only knew that nothing seemed to be the same any more.

A fortnight ago, his life had been his own, with everything planned out, everything just the way he wanted it.

Except for one thing.

He had wanted the Medrano Television Company and he had been determined to get it. And because of that one thing, it seemed that his life had been turned upside down.

No.

Raking his fingers through his hair, he massaged the muscles of his skull that always seemed to be so tight and tense these days.

It was not because of the television company that things didn't seem in control. It was because he had met Estrella Medrano. It was because of her that his life no longer felt as if it were his own.

He needed a drink.

On the way to the kitchen to find a large bottle of wine—the best his brother Joaquin's vineyard could produce—he noticed that the light on the telephone answering machine was flickering wildly and a glowing red number announced that he had five messages waiting.

That was hardly surprising. He had been preoccupied with so many things in the past couple of weeks that he had barely even touched base at his apartment. The time he hadn't spent working he had been at his father's home, or checking on Joaquin and how he was recovering from his recent accident. Pausing to press the 'play' button, he headed to the kitchen.

'Ramón, where are you, man?'

The sound of his other brother's voice made Ramón grin. A brand-new and hopelessly besotted father, Alex liked nothing better than to bore the rest of the family with tales of his tiny daughter, and just how wonderful she was. He'd missed a couple of bulletins this week, and clearly Alex was determined that he should catch up.

He'd opened the wine and was pouring it into a glass when the machine clicked, beeped, then moved on to the next message.

'Señor Dario?'

It was a female voice, low and slightly hesitant.

The bottle crashed down onto the worktop, Ramón's head coming up sharply, his face turning towards the kitchen door so that he could catch exactly what was being said.

The last time he'd heard that voice, it had been shouting at him down a long, elegant corridor in the Castillo Medrano.

I wouldn't marry you if my life and the future of mankind depended on it. The words echoed inside his head, clear as if they had just been spoken in reality.

And it's certainly going to take a whole lot more than just one kiss to make me change my mind.

Oh, damnation, now he'd missed what she'd said, his thoughts too occupied with the past. Just what could have brought Estrella Medrano to phone him here, when she had vowed never to see him again?

The third message, something unimportant and uninteresting about work, was already almost finished, and he was just about to press 'replay' for Estrella Medrano's message when the fourth one took over.

'Señor Dario? I've been trying to get in touch with you.'

She'd rung again!

Once more Ramón stood frozen, his wineglass halfway to his mouth, his mind busy, trying to work out just why the woman who had told him that he was tenth in the line of possible suitors for her hand—and she still wouldn't have him!—would now want to contact him so urgently.

The answering machine message told him nothing. Just that she had been trying to get in touch with him; she had called the flat before—which of course he knew—and she would try again.

She'd left no number, he noted. Nor had she suggested that he try to ring her.

Once again he was about to press replay when the doorbell rang, distracting him that way instead.

'I was just going to answer your call,' he said as he pulled the door open. 'There was no need for you to be so impatient about my getting back…'

The words faded from his tongue as he saw who stood outside, in the hallway beyond the door.

Not one of his brothers. Not his secretary who had left a message that she had some papers he needed to sign. Not even his young sister, Mercedes, who had clearly had something on her mind—some man on her mind—the last time he had seen her.

No one he was expecting.

Instead, it was the last person on earth he might have anticipated.

'You!'

Estrella Medrano stood on the landing, her shoulders

hunched rather defensively, her hands pushed into the pockets of the light linen jacket she wore with faded denim jeans and a soft white tee shirt.

'What are you doing here?'

'I thought you knew.'

'How the hell would I know?'

He knew his tone was too sharp. If he hadn't been able to hear it for himself, then the way she took half a step back, the set of her shoulders growing even more tense, would have told him that straight away. But he wasn't capable of controlling his tongue, or of putting on any carefully polite act just to please her. It had been a long, difficult day, at the end of a couple of long, difficult weeks and he was in no mood for playing social games with a woman who, the last time he had been in her company, had made it plain that she never wanted to see him again.

'You said you were going to get back to me.'

'That was before I knew it was you. I thought you were someone else,' he amended with pointed care. 'I was expecting my secretary.'

'I see. If it's inconvenient, I can go...'

'No.'

Now how the hell had that happened? He'd opened his mouth to say yes. Yes, it was terribly inconvenient. Yes, he wanted her to go. Yes, he'd meant it when he'd said that he wanted nothing more to do with her.

But somehow his subconscious had overridden his conscious thoughts and he had come out with the exact opposite.

'No—come in.'

In his own ears, his voice betrayed too much. It gave away the raw, unsettled feeling that had clawed at him in the first few moments of seeing this woman again. Just the sight of her brought back all the disturbed and restless nights he'd endured since he had walked out of the Castillo Medrano without looking back.

He had walked away but he hadn't been able to leave her behind, not in his thoughts. She had haunted his days and plagued his nights, the image of her beautiful face, her tall, slender form and long black hair filling his dreams. And those dreams had held the most potently erotic images he had ever known. Images of himself and this woman in bed together, of her warm, silken body pressed up against his, her long legs entwined with his, her mouth on his...

'No!' he said again, knowing that it was his own thoughts he was speaking to, not her, and had to hastily add on again, 'It's not inconvenient at all.'

The waft of her perfume as she walked past him, blended as it was with the light scent of her skin, was almost his undoing, making him swallow hard and force his mind to anything other than his body's immediate, hard reaction to her presence. He hoped to hell that she'd say what she had to say and get out of there fast.

As it was, he knew he was heading for another restless and sweat-soaked night. He took a hasty swallow of his wine in an effort to cool his rising temperature.

'Can I get you a drink?' he asked, suddenly remembering his manners.

'Thank you—yes.'

She looked almost as grateful as if he had thrown her a lifeline, which made him ask himself just why she was here. What was so important that she would overcome her dislike of him enough to come to his home? And how much polite small talk would they have to make before he could get her to say what it was?

'Red wine okay?'

'That would be perfect.'

'I'll get you a glass.'

To his horror she followed him into the kitchen when he had been hoping for a few much-needed seconds to pull himself together. His skin felt as if he were suffering from pins and needles, and his awareness of her was like a burn through every nerve.

The clinging white tee shirt outlined the rich swell of her breasts and emphasised the narrowness of her waist. And if her neat, pert bottom had been temptation enough under the slim-fitting black skirt, then in the tight, tight jeans it was a source of purely physical agony to look and not to be able to touch. Her long, lustrous black hair was caught up in a high pony-tail at the back of her head and the severely smooth hairstyle revealed her perfect features with dramatic clarity. Only the faintest touch of make-up enhanced the lush thickness of her eyelashes, the soft, seductive curves of her mouth.

He had thought that she was stunning in the simple elegance of her blouse and skirt, but the more casual clothes teased and tormented when their suggestion of informality blended with her careful physical distance. Wherever she moved, the traces of her scent lingered in the air, making his gut twist in instinctive reaction every time he breathed in.

Wine in hand, he led her through into the living room and settled her in a big, soft chair covered in caramel leather while he stayed on his feet, leaning against the carved wooden mantelpiece some distance away.

'So to what do I owe the honour of this visit?' he asked when it became obvious that she was not going to be the one to break the stiffly awkward silence that had formed between them. 'I take it there is a point to it? You didn't just come to see how the other half live?'

'Oh, no—it wasn't that at all.'

'Then would you mind telling me what it is?'

How—just how—did she answer that? Estrella asked herself privately. This whole idea had seemed so amazing, so scarily impossible, but at the same time so very right when she had thought of it. But as soon as the door had opened and she had come face to face with Ramón once again, every last trace of any sort of confidence had vanished, leaving her feeling as if an earthquake had just opened up a huge chasm beneath her feet and she were barely clinging onto the sides by her nails.

She had forgotten how tall he was, how imposing, and, even though she was prepared for it, the impact of his devastating dark looks was like a punch in the face, making her senses reel. He had clearly just got back from the office or somewhere similar and the silvery grey shirt he wore together with the trousers of another impeccably tailored suit—black this time—emphasised and enhanced the lean, hard lines of his powerfully masculine frame.

The suit jacket had been discarded somewhere, the burgundy and black tie tugged loose and a single button at the neck of the shirt pulled open and left unfastened. In the space it revealed, an expanse of long, tautly muscled throat was exposed, the sleek skin tanned warmly golden by the sun.

Just to look at him dried her mouth. And although she knew that nerves were partly the cause of it, she was painfully aware of the fact that there were other, less fearful causes to contend with. Her pulse thudded at her temples and she knew it wasn't just apprehension that made it race in that way.

'Well?' Ramón enquired cynically, clearly impatient at her hesitation. 'Why are you here?'

'I—I needed to talk to you.'

'What about—another marriage proposal?'

Estrella's throat closed up sharply at the question and she

had to swallow hard to ease the painful tightness and con-
striction.

'I...' she began but her voice cracked and failed her. Even
another hasty sip of wine did nothing to ease the situation.

'What is this, Doña Medrano? Has your father sent you
to try and get me to change my mind? Or perhaps you
couldn't bring yourself to tell him that yet another man had
turned you down and so he wants to know what my answer
will be.'

Estrella winced inwardly at the sting of his sarcasm and
tried to sit up straighter, forcing herself to meet the scathing
silvery gleam of his narrowed eyes.

'My father doesn't know that I'm here.'

That surprised him. Just for a second he let it show in his
face, his eyes opening wide, his head going back slightly.
But a moment later he had himself back under control and
a coolly assessing, guarded look masked his carved features.

'He doesn't? So where does he think you are?'

'With friends. I told him I was going to visit my old
school friend in town.'

'And you neglected to tell him that this "old school
friend" was in fact me?'

'Mmm.'

It was all that she could manage, her voice deserting her
again. She knew how it must seem, it all sounded so underhand and cloak-and-daggerish, and she could see from
the look on his face that he was both deeply suspicious and
slightly intrigued, in spite of himself.

She would concentrate on that 'intrigued', she told herself. At least if she had piqued his curiosity he was unlikely
to actually throw her out until she had explained. When she
had decided to come here, she hadn't really known whether
he would even let her in the door. She had had visions of
being dismissed without a word, of having the door

slammed in her face before she had a chance to explain. When she had anticipated that sort of reception, this was progress.

'Even more interesting,' Ramón murmured with deceptive silkiness. 'Not only do you turn up out of the blue, when you swore you never wanted to see me again, but you also lie to your *papá* in order to do so. Which makes me wonder just why this visit is so important to you.'

It was now or never. Estrella swallowed some more wine in the hope it would give her courage. She hadn't actually decided to go through with this yet. The idea that she had come up with had seemed like the perfect answer in the middle of the night, in the darkness of her room at the *castillo*. But here, in the light of day, in Ramón's elegant apartment, and with the man himself towering above her as he stood beside the big, carved fireplace, all her convictions had deserted her. And the daring—the audacity—that had brought her here today was rapidly seeping away from her as if there were holes in her toes through which all her strength was leaking out.

But she remembered how she had planned to lead into it. She'd go with that for now and see what happened. If it didn't work out, or his mood changed, she could still leave with the major part of her idea left unsaid. If she took one step at a time she could test out the water as she went.

The thought restored something of her mental courage and her voice was surprisingly strong when she answered him.

'I—came to offer you an apology.'

That surprised him. It was clearly the last thing he was expecting. He stilled abruptly with his glass half raised to his mouth and stared at her fixedly across the top of it, cool grey eyes locking with uncertain deep brown ones. Then abruptly he shook his head.

'I don't think I heard right,' he said, his voice sounding rough at the edges. 'I thought you said—'

'That I've come to apologise—I have!'

Clearly he didn't believe her. The look he turned on her was frankly sceptical, ice seeming to form in the storm-cloud depths of his eyes.

'Apologise for what?' he demanded.

Some of Estrella's hard-won composure slipped away again and she thought about taking another fortifying sip of wine. But the fear that it would get caught in the knot in her throat, choking her, made her rethink and replace the glass on the coffee-table in front of her.

'For my—for my father's behaviour—and mine the other day—when you came to the castle. We should never have—I feel really bad about it.'

Wide, dark eyes went to his face, scrutinising the hard cast of his features in the hope of seeing that he understood. But the strong-boned face was unyielding, his expression still set hard as rock, and she couldn't see even a flicker of response in the opaque, silvery stare.

'I—I'm sorry.'

She wished he would speak—say something, anything! But instead he finished what was left in his wineglass and moved to throw himself down on the huge settee that matched the armchair in which she sat, perched uncomfortably on its edge. In contrast, Ramón stretched himself out in totally comfortable abandon, his shining dark head resting on the pale leather, his legs out in front of him, crossed at the ankle above his highly polished handmade boots.

But his eyes remained watchful, sharply assessing. He formed his fingers into a steeple and pressed them against his mouth, studying her over the top of them.

'Ramón...' she began, unable to bear the silence any longer, but he cut in on her without apology.

'Say that again,' he commanded harshly. 'What you said just now—say it again.'

What did he want—proof of her honesty? Or did he merely want to humiliate her by making her repeat over and over again the embarrassing reason why she had come?

'That I want to apologise? I do. I really do. My father was wrong to ask you—'

'He did more than ask.'

'I know he made your marrying me the condition for selling you the TV company. He should never have done that. And I...'

Her nerves almost failed her and she had to pause, draw in a deep, calming breath and let it out again before she could find the strength to continue.

'I should never have reacted in the way I did.'

Still those cool grey eyes watched her, slightly narrowed again, fixed on her face, noting every change of expression, each tiny flicker of emotion that crossed her fine-boned features.

'I could almost believe you mean that,' he said at last.

'I do!'

She wanted him to believe that. She needed him to believe it. If he didn't, then the rest of her idea was ruined from the start.

'I do mean it,' she assured him, leaning forward in her seat, her face towards his, her eyes fixed on his. 'I hope you can believe that.'

The faint pause, the break in her speech, was because she hoped that he would speak. To give him time to cut in and say: 'I can—I do believe that.'

But Ramón did nothing of the sort. Instead he simply sat where he was, grey eyes locking with hers, and he watched and he waited. Until his silence began to tug hard on her nerves, making her shift uncomfortably in her seat.

'My father should never have put those conditions on you—no matter what his reasons. And I should have come right out and told you that I knew—well, that I guessed— he was up to his tricks again. I should have let you know...'

She was burbling, and she knew it, but there was nothing she could do to stop herself. Ramón's silence had got to her and she had to do something, anything to fill it.

'I should have said something from the first.'

'But you didn't.'

'No—no, I didn't.'

'Care to tell me why?'

Did she want to tell him? Was she ready to tell him? Even more importantly, how much was she ready to tell him? Estrella couldn't answer the questions in her own thoughts, so she had no idea how to answer his.

'I—' she tried, but then nerves struck, her mind shut down and became a total blank. So instead of speaking, she reached for her wineglass and downed what was left in it.

'I'd prefer it if you didn't get drunk,' Ramón commented dryly. 'I really don't think it would help my case with your father if I had to take you home half out of your mind on alcohol.'

'I'm not drunk!' she protested indignantly, but she could feel the hot colour rushing into her cheeks.

'Halfway there. So tell me, is what you have to say so terrible that you have to be drunk to admit to it?'

If she was drunk, it would be easier, Estrella acknowledged inwardly. Perhaps some degree of inebriation would make it less difficult to tell this man that she hadn't been able to get him out of her mind since she had first met him. That he had walked through her dreams every night, and images of him had plagued her thoughts by day. She had tried to push them away, tried to think of anything but him, but that had only seemed to make matters worse. All she was aware of was the man she was trying not to think of and she might just as well have indulged her imagination and let it run riot.

But that was more than she dared to admit, at least with those cool grey eyes assessing every move she made, every word she uttered.

Hopelessly embarrassed, she set the glass down on the table and stared fixedly at it, unable to meet his eyes.

'Well, Doña Medrano?' Ramón questioned and the deliberate provocation of that 'Doña' sparked her temper, making her head lift defiantly, and pushing her into unguarded speech.

'You know perfectly well what started all this! Everyone knows! That's why my father plays these games—why he tries to bribe people—or coerce them—to marry me. You've known that all the time. You were the one who brought Carlos into things last time.'

I'm not so desperate that I would want Carlos Perea's cast-offs, he had said, and the words had hurt far more than the angry lash of his tongue. Now, looking into his cold, set face, she saw the same blazing contempt, the same cruel disgust.

'Ah—so it is Perea that we're talking about. I wondered when we'd get to the real truth. What is all this about—are you trying to claim that Carlos Perea never happened? That the story about your affair is just fiction?'

Oh, how she wished she could.

'No,' she muttered, low and miserable. 'I'm not going to claim that. I couldn't—it wouldn't be true. Carlos—Carlos happened...'

'So are you going to explain to me why you threw yourself at a married man, how you enticed him so that he left his wife and—was it three children?—for you?'

'Two,' Estrella muttered defensively. 'It was only two.'

'And I suppose you think that makes a difference?'

'I don't think anything makes a difference.'

Nothing eased her conscience, that was for sure. And nothing, it seemed, was going to restore her good name and her reputation ever again.

'No,' Ramón agreed cynically, suddenly moving up and out of his seat as if he could no longer stand to be so close to her. 'I don't suppose any of it mattered to you—the fact that he had a wife and kids at home, and that he broke all of their hearts by running after you. That just wasn't important to you, was it? You got what you wanted and you didn't care how much it cost anyone else.'

She would have thought that it was impossible for her heart to sink any lower or for the bitter memories of her past mistake to haunt her in any more painful ways. But she had never felt so low, so unwanted, so totally cheap and tawdry as she did now. Even when she had found out the truth about Carlos, it hadn't made her feel quite so sordid, so tainted as the deep, dark scorn in Ramón Dario's voice did now.

And she couldn't take any more of it. She pushed herself to her feet, forced herself to keep her head high, her eyes blazing defiance into his.

'It wasn't like that, Señor Dario!'

To her delight she actually managed to control her voice, to stop it from shaking, though the effort made it sound painfully cold and shrill. But right now that was the lesser of two evils, she decided miserably.

'It wasn't like that at all! But then, I don't expect you to believe that. I did wonder if you were different, but it seems I was wrong. Of course I was wrong! You're not any different—you're just like all the others—like my father...'

'Hell, no!'

She'd caught him on the raw there. He was furious—

coldly, blazingly angry. The grey eyes were molten, his nostrils flaring, and there were white marks etched around his nose and mouth.

'Hell, yes!' she flung at him. 'You're so like him it isn't true! You just see what you want to see; believe what you want to believe. You don't want to look behind things to see what might actually be the truth!'

'Are you saying—?'

'I'm saying nothing—except goodnight.'

Turning swiftly, she snatched up her bag, gripping the handles so tight that her knuckles turned white. She might just make it to the door. If she was quick and she was strong.

'Goodnight, Señor Dario,' she managed through gritted teeth. 'Thank you for the wine. I wish I could say that it's been nice—but I prefer not to lie.'

She thought he was going to let her go. When he watched in silence as she stalked across the room, she believed that that was it. That she'd blown her chance, burned her bridges, and that any hopes of carrying out her plan would have to be abandoned once and for all. There was no hope at all that he was going to help her now.

But it wasn't that thought that had the tears pushing at the backs of her eyes, burning them cruelly. It was the knowledge that once again she'd failed to convince someone that she was not how they believed her to be. And, almost complete stranger though he was, she hated the thought that Ramón too had joined the ranks of those who condemned her without hearing her story.

She hadn't had much hope when she'd arrived at his apartment earlier that evening, but she'd had a tiny ray of optimism. At least there had been a chance that he might listen.

Now there was nothing.

The walk across the room seemed to take for ever. Every

step felt as if she were ploughing through mud, her legs were as feeble as if they were stuffed with cotton wool. And the fight against tears blurred her vision so that she could barely see a thing in front of her.

But she was not going to look back. She was not going to hesitate. Not going to show a sign of weakness.

'Estrella.'

Ramón's voice came when she was least expecting it, and at first it was so soft that, concentrating on getting through this haze of misery and out of the door, she wasn't sure if she had heard it or simply imagined the sound in her head. But then he spoke again, and this time there was no mistaking it.

'Estrella, don't go.'

It was the first time that he had used her name, Estrella registered as her footsteps slowed, stilled. The first time he had ever said 'Estrella', and the realisation was like the stab of a stiletto as she suddenly thought that she had never heard it sound so right, so perfect. Her heart clenched at the thought that this might be the one, the only time she would hear him say it.

But she still couldn't bring herself to turn round or face him. She was too afraid of what she might see in his eyes, and what he might be able to read from hers. If she had to go, then she wanted to go now.

If she hesitated, or looked back, then she might never be able to make herself move on again.

CHAPTER FOUR

IT WAS the first time he had ever spoken her name, Ramón realised on a wave of shock. The first time he had ever personalised her so much as to call her by her given name rather than thinking of her as Alfredo Medrano's daughter, or the more sarcastic Doña Medrano.

Or the woman he had been expected to ask to marry him.

It was a shock. A real slap-in-the-face, punch-in-the-guts shock.

Had he really not ever seen the person in this woman? He had kissed her, dreamed of her, fantasised about her—but had he ever really and truly seen her?

Now she had frozen, still facing the door, turned away from him. All he could see was her tall, slender back, the curving hips and long legs. There was the silken fall of her jet-black hair. But he couldn't see her face.

Had he really ever seen her face? Had he really ever seen her?

Who was Estrella Medrano? Who was this woman he had practically been ordered to marry—so arrogantly, so auto-cratically that he had been set against her from the start?

'Don't go,' he repeated, more firmly this time. 'Don't walk out like this. Stay.'

Slowly, so slowly, she pivoted on one high heel and turned in a semi-circle until she was facing him. Her eyes looked suspiciously bright, glistening in the deep rays of sunset that flooded through the huge windows, and her face seemed different. Paler and drawn in, more delicate somehow.

Or was that just another thing he had never seen before?

'Stay?' she echoed softly, questioningly. 'Why?'

She looked as wary as a hunted animal, watching him through wide, apprehensive eyes as if she feared he would pounce suddenly and dangerously.

'Have you eaten?'

This time she simply shook her head, not seeming to trust her voice to answer him.

'Neither have I—and we both need something to offset the wine.'

Another silent movement of her head, this time a nod, was her only answer.

'Okay.'

To get to the kitchen he had to walk past her and she watched him mutely, her pale face set into wary, uncertain lines.

He didn't like the way that made him feel. He'd never had a woman react to him in this way. And there had been plenty of women over the years. Women who had been easy to talk to, easy to charm. But this one was as wary as a feral cat. One moment she was curled up on a chair, smooth and sleek and almost comfortable. The next she was hissing and scratching like a little tiger, brown eyes flashing fire and that proud head up high.

'I'm not going to hurt you.'

He felt obliged to say it. Anything to make her relax.

'No,' she said in a strangely mangled little voice. 'I don't suppose you intend to.'

'And just what is that supposed to mean?'

He was directly opposite her now, facing her head-on, and he could see the cloudiness of those beautiful eyes, the tautness of the muscles of her face.

'Estrella…' he prompted harshly when she hesitated to give him an answer.

'It means—' she said, meeting his eyes fiercely even though he could see the faint tremor in her slim body as she fought for control. 'It means that sometimes you're just like all the others. You only see what's in front of your face.'

'All the others? Do you mean the other men your father tried to get to marry you? The other men he wanted to buy?'

It made his stomach curdle to be lumped together with them all like this. To be just one name on a list.

'Damn you, Estrella—I'm not like that!'

'No?' she challenged, folding her arms in front of her, one small, booted foot tapping angrily on the polished wood of the floor. 'No? Are you sure?'

'Of course I'm sure! They all knew they could get something from your father. They asked you to marry them.'

'So what's different? How are you not like them? Tell me what you were doing in that room—why was I sent to speak to you? What were you going to do?'

'I sure as hell wasn't going to do what your father asked.'

'You—you really weren't?'

'Didn't you listen to a word I said? No, I was not! You want to know the difference between us—between me and those other men your father bought? The point is that he managed to buy them! They asked you to marry them. I didn't.'

'Because—'

'No.'

Ramón lifted a hand and brought it down between them in a hard, slashing movement as if he was physically cutting off the conversation.

'Not because I didn't get the chance. Or because you rounded on me like a spitting cat. Or because we fought so hard that I changed my mind and thought the better of it. I didn't ask you because I didn't want to!'

He wouldn't have done anything Alfredo Medrano had

wanted, not with the insults the old man had flung at him still echoing in his thoughts.

'My company is not for the likes of you,' Medrano had tossed at him. 'The land on which the television station is built has been in the Medrano family for years. I'll not sell it to some jumped-up nobody who from what I hear doesn't even have the right to the name he bears, and who just happens to have made his first million.'

He had actually turned and had been walking out, Ramón remembered, when the old snake had offered his other suggestion—that he marry Estrella and so gain the television company that way.

'I was never going to ask you from the start. Not even when he offered me the company for half the asking price if I'd take you along with it.'

If she had looked stunned before, then she looked positively dazed now. Her face had no colour at all in it apart from the deep pools of her eyes, the pink curves of her mouth. He had moved closer as he spoke, so close that he could see the faint indentations in her lips where her sharp white teeth had dug into them, worrying away at them.

Just for a moment he was tempted to lift a finger and smooth it over her mouth, to try to ease away the marks of the damage she had done. But she wasn't going to tolerate that, he knew. If he tried, she would probably turn and run, out the door before he had time to breathe.

'But—I know how much you wanted that TV company.'

'Yes,' Ramón admitted, nodding his head to emphasise the word. 'Yes, I wanted it. At the time I thought it was the deal I most wanted in the world.'

Just for a moment he allowed himself to remember how much the deal had meant to him.

'And is there nothing else that would give you the same satisfaction?'

'Nothing else that matches it. I hated the thought that I'd lost it—still do.'

'Why is that?'

Ramón sighed, pushed both hands through the gleaming sleekness of his hair.

'Ah, well that's a long story.'

'I've got all night.'

She sounded as if she meant it. And the weird thing was that he felt he could tell her. That he could explain something of the way he'd been feeling, something of his family's complicated history.

'Do you really want to hear this? If so, perhaps we'd better sit down again.'

She followed him back to the fireplace, each of them settling in the places they had occupied just a few moments before. Ramón reached for the wine bottle, refilled their glasses then pushed one towards Estrella. Taking a long swallow from the other, he hunted for the words.

'To understand this, you need to know something about my family.'

'I know that your mother was English and your father—'

'If you mean Reuben Dario then he was not my father. Not my biological father.'

Her start of surprise showed that this was news to her.

'Then who…?'

'Juan Alcolar.'

'Of the Alcolar Corporation?'

'And more. That's right.'

He stared down into his glass, swirling the rich red wine around in the bottom of it.

'He and my mother had an affair and I was the result. But she was married to my—to Reuben at the time. So he made her promise never to tell.'

'So you grew up thinking that Reuben Dario was your father?'

Ramón nodded slowly.

'I was even registered as his. But I couldn't have been. Reuben couldn't have children of his own.'

'And your mother never told you?'

'She never got a chance. She died when I was tiny. But she left me a letter to read when I was twenty-one. That was when I found out.'

'How did you feel?'

Ramón shot her a swift sidelong glance from those silvery eyes.

'How do you think I felt? How would you feel if you suddenly discovered that your *papá* wasn't really your father?'

Estrella clearly considered it, then shook her head. She looked totally bemused, Ramón reflected, but she couldn't feel anything like the way that he'd been left reeling when he'd found out the truth.

'Lost,' she managed.

'Which is exactly how I felt. I didn't know where I belonged—who I was. Who my family was. Reuben and I had never really got along. We were too unlike each other—miles apart. I wanted to work in the media and he wanted me to do something sensible—become an accountant like him. We fought about it endlessly. That was something I understood better when I knew where I really came from. When I realised that my father was in fact Don Juan Alcolar.'

Once more he slanted one of those glances in her direction.

'So you see,' he went on, his tone darkly dry, 'your father might have been more inclined to hand his precious company over to me if he'd known that I was the son of another of the great Catalan families. One whose name and title goes back even further than the Medranos. And someone who's made a fortune in the media.'

'Is that why you wanted the company—so you could be part of the Alcolar empire?'

Ramón shook his dark head emphatically, rejection of her question in his eyes, his face.

'No way. I wanted it so that I could have something of my own that would not have come from the Alcolar fortunes but from my hard work. When I went to find my father— my real father—he welcomed me into his family. I think he was thrilled to have a son who was involved in the same business as him. Joaquin has no interest in it. He took himself out into the country and runs his own vineyard and wine-exporting business. And Alex—well, Alex took on another role in the corporation.'

'Alex?' Estrella questioned curiously and saw Ramón's mouth quirk up sharply at one corner.

'Alex is another brother—half-brother—by another woman. I warned you it was complicated.'

Estrella could only shake her head and reach for her glass. It was complicated and quite frankly it stunned her. Ramón's father had been unfaithful to his wife with two other women—had fathered children by them—and yet he had emerged from the situation with his reputation unscathed. While she had innocently, stupidly, blindly become involved with a married man, and as a result she had been branded a scarlet woman ever since.

But then, of course, this was Spain. And Spain was a man's country. Look at the way people spoke of Carlos now. As someone whose behaviour they understood—he was a man, and he had had his head turned by a capricious and irresponsible young girl. But then they had all got to know him again in the time before she had returned from the convent boarding school, the exclusive finishing college her father had thought would turn her into the lady he wanted as his daughter. And then Carlos had died so tragically.

'So—the television company would have been yours. Not a part of the Alcolar Corporation.'

'Exactly. It would have been just about the only thing that I knew was truly mine—not Alcolar, not Dario. Mine. My father would have given me part of the Alcolar Corporation but that wasn't what I wanted. What I wanted was to match up to him—to my real father—in the world in which he moves. And, of course, being a Medrano business, it would also bring with it something of the "old Spain", the Catalan heritage that Juan Alcolar values perhaps even more than your father.'

One long finger tapped a restless percussion on the side of his glass, betraying the state of his feelings far more than any words.

'So now perhaps you'll see why I wanted it so much.'

If that didn't give her the perfect opening to tell him just what had been in her mind when she'd come here, then nothing else would, Estrella told herself, drawing in a deep breath and straightening her shoulders as if suddenly facing up to something she had to do.

If she was ever going to do it, then it was now or never.

'So what if I told you that you didn't have to lose it?'

There, now she'd said it, Estrella acknowledged, feeling the cold touch of fear zigzagging down her spine so that she couldn't hold back a shiver in spite of the setting sun burning beyond the windows. As soon as she'd seen his reaction, when he'd admitted just how much he'd wanted the deal with her father, she'd known that she'd never get another chance. There couldn't be a better opening, any more of a lead-in to the reason for her being here in the first place.

But she couldn't believe she'd had the nerve, that she'd actually come out and said the words, and, to judge from the expression on his face, the way his black brows had suddenly snapped together in a sceptical frown, neither could Ramón.

'What?' he said, his tone revealing his shock. 'What are you talking about?'

'I'm asking what you'd do if you knew that there was a way that you didn't have to lose out on the deal you wanted. A way that the television company can be yours after all.'

'And precisely how would I do that?'

'H-how?'

The word came out as an embarrassing squeak. Estrella's mouth and throat were painfully dry and she tried to swallow to ease the sensation but with no effect. Her vocal cords seemed to have seized up and she couldn't find the strength to answer him.

'Estrella? What the devil are you saying? That just isn't possible. You know what happened. Your father threw the whole deal back in my face.'

'But I think you could persuade him to change his mind.'

'You'd have to be mad to think so!' Ramón dismissed the idea scornfully. 'He said he wouldn't sell.'

'Except under one condition.'

Surprisingly, now it seemed that her voice had come back, stronger and clearer than ever. It was as if, once she had got over the shock of actually hearing herself say the words that had started her on this crazy course of action, suddenly all the thoughts and the plans, all the arguments she'd given herself in favour of coming here, had buoyed her up, giving her the strength she needed. She actually sounded calm and confident, sure of her direction.

It was Ramón's reaction that she couldn't even begin to predict.

'One condition,' he echoed now and the words were full of total disbelief darkened by an undercurrent of angry rejection. 'But, Estrella, you know what that condition was. He wanted—'

'He wanted you to marry me,' she finished for him when he broke off, shaking his dark head in disbelief. 'My father said that he would only sell you the company if you would agree to marry me.'

'Are you saying that you're agreeing to that? That you'd go along with his demands?'

Was she saying that? Was she really prepared to go through with this? She'd thought so when she'd come here. It was what had been in her mind.

Estrella drew on all the strength she could find.

'That's exactly what I'm saying.'

'You want me to marry you?'

'Yes. Yes, I do.'

CHAPTER FIVE

'RAMÓN—please!'

It was all that she could manage. She could read the rejection of everything she had said in his eyes, in every set, hard muscle in his face. If he had flung the suggestion right back at her then, he couldn't have made it any more plain that he wanted nothing to do with the idea at all.

'This is a joke, right?'

'N-no.'

The confidence that had buoyed her up was ebbing, leaving her feeling lost and desperately deflated. She'd staked all her hopes on one thing, played the only card she had in her hand, and it seemed that she had lost everything.

'No joke.'

'You mean it?'

He flung himself to his feet and, as he had done that day in the castle, he whirled away from her, pacing across the room to stand by the big windows, staring out at the rapidly darkening sky, the lights of the city coming on below. Then just as abruptly he turned and strode back, the sound of his steps on the polished wooden floor echoing the uneven, jerky beats of her heart.

'Why the devil would you even suggest this? What sort of madness—?'

'It's not madness.'

Desperation made her insert the words into his angry speech, making him break off and stare at her as if she had suddenly grown two heads.

Needing to be able to meet him more equally, eye to eye

rather than feeling overpowered by the way he towered over her, she forced herself to her feet, actually took a couple of steps forward, towards him.

'It's not madness, Ramón! It could work—you'd get what you want and I...'

'That's the part I don't understand. Just what will you get out of this?'

'My freedom.'

Just two simple words but they meant so much.

'Freedom?'

'Yes. You've seen how it is. You've seen what my father's like—how he's desperate for me to be married—to restore the good name of the family that he thinks I sullied so badly.'

'You seem to be dealing with that just fine from what I can see. You're just turning down everyone who asks.'

'But you can't see everything.'

Her legs suddenly feeling weak beneath her, Estrella moved back to the big leather chair by the fireplace and perched on one thickly padded arm. Ramón watched her go, leaning back against the doorjamb and folding his arms across his broad chest.

'You're not there when I'm alone with him; when I have to listen to his lectures, put up with his rages. When he tells me what a disappointment I am to him, how I've shamed him—shamed the family. And he won't give up. He'll just keep on trying to get me married, getting these men to propose to me—paying them. And you're not there when they come to propose. When they eye me up like a horse at an auction, wondering if my breeding stock is worth putting up with my appalling reputation. I'm so tired of it, Ramón. It's humiliating. I hate it.'

'Then do something about it.'

'That's what I want to do.'

She tried a smile but there was no softening of the hard cast of his features.

'I want it to stop. And as far as I can see the only way to make it stop for good is to give my father what he wants. He wants me married. So if I get married—if I have a ring on my finger and the respectable name that goes with it, then people will forget the past. My father will forget the past.'

'But you'll have to live with the present.'

'I know. Do you think I haven't thought about this? That I haven't gone over and over it in my head until I thought I was going completely mad? Do you think I haven't tried to come up with some other solution?'

'But why me?'

'I told you…'

But he wanted more. She could see that in his face. There was more but she wasn't at all sure she could tell him that now. Not now, with the space of the room between them, the expanse of the floor seeming to stretch out like some wide, gaping chasm with each of them on a different side of it.

She couldn't tell him now.

'I told you…' she repeated forlornly.

'Tell me again.'

Ramón pushed himself away from the wall and covered the space between them in five swift strides. He came to where she was sitting and leaned over her, one hand on the high back of the chair, the other on the padded arm where she sat. His position enclosed her completely, trapping her; she was unable to move.

She risked one swift glance up into the dark, shuttered face, the ice of his eyes, and couldn't take any more. Dropping her own gaze, she tried to stare down at her knees but only succeeded in making herself sharply, painfully aware of the way that his body was surrounding hers, putting her into a cage made of the long, powerful limbs, the hard, solid wall of his torso. His arms were braced against the chair, long muscles stretched taut to take his weight. His body was so close to her face, the heat of his skin, the tangy scent of some lime-based cologne tormenting her nostrils.

His hips were against her knees, the narrow leather belt at his waist within inches of the hands that rested on her thighs. If she was just to reach out, ever so slightly, she could touch him...

But even as the thought slid into her mind Ramón's hand came under her chin, forcing her face up with a rough, jerky movement.

And this was so much worse. Because now, if she looked up, she was drowning in the silvery pools of his eyes. If she tried to drop her gaze then it rested on the beautiful, sensual shape of his mouth. On the lips that had kissed her only once but that she had dreamed of ever since. That kiss had driven her insane with wanting and it was the wanting that surfaced, hot and hungry now, just remembering.

'Tell me what you'll get out of this,' Ramón commanded, the harsh, grating tone slicing through the sensual haze that clouded her mind.

'I told you—my freedom. I'll get my freedom.'

'And that's enough? Enough to make you tie yourself to a stranger?'

'Not just any stranger—you.'

Ramón's breath hissed in through his teeth in a sound that expressed his struggle for control.

'And why me? I've asked this before, Estrella, and I'll keep on asking it until you give me an answer. Why me?'

Why me?

Oh, how did she answer that? With the truth. It was the only way. So although her stomach quailed deep inside, her nerves twisting into tight, agonising knots, she swallowed hard, forced herself to meet his eyes, and told him.

'Because of what you said earlier. Because you weren't going to ask me when my father wanted you to. You walked out on the deal you wanted—that's why. And—and…'

'And?' Ramón prompted when she couldn't go on, the words refusing to come past the blockage in her throat. 'And what?'

'And this.' Estrella sighed. 'And this…'

Raising her head, she pressed her mouth to his, kissing him softly.

Just for a second she felt his shock, the hardening of his body in resistance, and a terrible arrow of fear streaked through her brain at the thought that maybe she'd got this completely wrong. That her memories of that first kiss on the day they had met had been all wrong, a mistake, a delusion she had dreamed or her imagination had created out her own longings. But a moment later she heard his sigh and his mouth softened against hers, taking the kiss and returning it easily and lightly.

It was nothing like that first kiss. In fact it was the exact opposite of that hard, almost cruel taking of her mouth, but gentle as it was it woke the same feelings, the same burning hunger as that moment. In the space of a heartbeat it was as if the first, faint smoulder of awareness had ignited, flaring into an all-encompassing flame that swept through her, carrying her into another world. One of heat and hunger and pure sensation that made her head spin wildly.

Oh thank heaven, was the only thought that slid through the burning haze in her mind before her thought processes closed down completely. Thank heaven that she hadn't got it wrong. That she hadn't been imagining things and the wild, fierce hunger really was there between them. The wild, fierce hunger that she remembered, that she had dreamed of knowing again. The hunger that had driven her into this crazy scheme in the first place and that she prayed would see them through.

And this…

The words were still sounding in Ramón's head when her lips first touched his but they were the last reasonably coherent idea he was capable of forming. From the moment that he felt Estrella's mouth on his, tasted her on his lips, on his tongue, it was as if some huge explosion in his brain had short-circuited all his thought processes, turning them into a blazing, molten mess that could register nothing but heat.

His body was hot. His thoughts were hot. His hunger was hotter than any of them.

His fingers closed around the tops of her arms, encircling them almost totally as he hauled her up from her seat on the chair and crushed her tight against him. Adjusting his position a little and angling his head just so, he managed to change the emphasis of the kiss so that instead of her kissing him, now he was kissing her, taking her mouth with all the force of the passion that had him in its grip.

The heat in his veins made his blood pound until the sound of his own pulse was like thunder raging at his temples. There was only one thing he was aware of in the world and that was Estrella. Estrella with her smooth skin and her slender body. Estrella with the long, flowing black hair.

That hair was caught up in the pony-tail at the back of her head, frustrating him when he wanted to run his fingers through it. With a swift tugging movement he pulled off the band that held it tight, discarding it somewhere on the floor as his hand combed down the long, silky strands.

The feel of its softness against his face, the faint fragrance of some herbal shampoo, added fuel to the flames of hunger that were building inside him. Tangling his hands in the fall

of her hair, he twisted it slightly, curving his palm against
the shape of her skull, holding her where he wanted her,
with her mouth locked with his.

'Ramón…'

It was a gasping cry as she dragged in a much-needed
breath, and somehow the sound of her voice acted on him
like a trigger, bringing him instantly to the point where kissing was not enough. Where he needed more. So much more.

He needed all of her. All she had to give. And he needed
it now.

The linen jacket was tugged off her shoulders, down her
arms and dropped onto the floor at their feet. The white,
clinging tee shirt followed it swiftly, the sudden rush of the
scent of her warm skin, her heady perfume assailing him
with a force that made his head swim. His mouth was hungry for the knowledge of her skin, for the feel of its satin
texture under his lips, the taste of it on his tongue.

Her hands were on his thigh; at his waist. The lightness
of her touch was almost an agony for him when he wanted
so much more. He groaned against her skin, kissing his way
down from the responsive mouth, along the line of her jaw,
her neck. He paused for a second or two at the spot where
a pulse throbbed at the base of her throat, kissing there too,
stroking it with his tongue, so that he felt under his lips the
way that her pulse kicked up again, beating ever faster than
before.

'You taste wonderful…so good.'

He felt her flesh quiver under the words, heard her sighing
moan of acquiescence, and couldn't hold back the laugh of
triumph and delight that bubbled up inside him. More kisses
took him to where the delicate peach-coloured strap of her
bra lay just by the smooth, rounded curve of her shoulder.
With his hands busy on her waist, tracing patterns on her

torso, he used his teeth to tug at the silky fabric until it slid down over her arm, the lacy cup of the bra lowering too.

'Touch me…touch me…' Estrella moaned in a litany of need, her voice thick with an echo of the aching hunger that suffused every inch of his body. 'Touch me…really touch me.'

Ramón laughed again, taking those slow, tantalising kisses even lower, across the scented slope of her breast and down, down towards the sensitive spot where her swollen pink nipple pressed against the peach lace.

'Is this what you want, *querida?*' he muttered as his mouth grazed the erect tip. 'Or this?'

This time his tongue slid around it, drawing tiny, erotic patterns that made her shudder in uncontrolled response.

'Or this…'

His lips closed over the darkened nipple, drawing it totally into his mouth and alternately suckling it and swirling his tongue around it until she was crying aloud in agonised delight.

He'd never known a woman so responsive to him. Never experienced the hot intensity of need that felt as if molten gold were flowing along his veins instead of blood. Estrella's head was thrown back, her black hair falling in a wild stream down her narrow back, her body arched against the thickly padded arm of the chair.

He couldn't wait a moment longer. He had to have her now. Had to know what it felt to be inside her, to be connected with her in the most complete, most total, most intimate way.

His hands fumbled blindly at the fastening of her jeans, snapping it open and wrenching down the denim and the slip of satin and lace beneath in one swift, forceful movement. His mouth moved lower too, kissing a line from her breasts, past her navel and into the dark cluster of curls at the juncture of her thighs, feeling her writhe and tighten beneath him as his kisses reached the most feminine part of her.

Her fingers were in his hair, clutching and tugging, alternately pulling him closer then almost, but not quite, pushing him away as if she just couldn't take the intimacy or the pleasure any longer.

They were sliding down from the chair, tumbling onto the floor, the polished wood cool against bared skin. And as they went Estrella was tugging at his shirt, yanking it free at his waist, wrenching the buttons open as rapidly as she could. Hunger made her fingers clumsy and he heard the fine fabric tear at one point but couldn't give a damn. What she wanted, he wanted too and that was the feeling of flesh against flesh, without the barrier of any clothing.

Eagerly helping her, shrugging off the ruined shirt and flinging it across the room, he muttered against her ear.

'Estrella, *mi estrella*. My beautiful star. Sweetheart—we can't do this...'

Can't do this? The words were like a dash of cold water in Estrella's heated brain.

Can't do this?

How could he say that now? Now when she was so close to the edge her body was screaming in its need. When she knew that she had to have Ramón make love to her or die from the burn of frustration. When all her thoughts, all her needs, all her fantasies were concentrated on just one thing...

'Can't?'

Her voice was hoarse with need.

'Can't? But—' She protested again and heard his soft laughter warm her cheek.

'Not here, *mi ángel*. Not here. The floor—'

He broke off on a gasp as, refusing to listen to his protests, she clamped her fingers on the buckle of his belt and tugged it open. Below it, the force of his erection strained against the fine material of his trousers.

'Estrella!' It was a moan of protest and defeat all blended into one. 'I'm trying to think of you!'

'And I'm saying I don't care!'

She had found the zip now, and wrenched it down so that the heated hardness of him spilled out, making him groan aloud in sensual relief.

'But the floor—too hard. My room...'

He was fighting to get the words out as she caressed him, taking the strength of him in her hand.

'The bed—'

'No.'

Estrella didn't want to move. She didn't want to risk any change of place or any pause in the blazing urgency that had her in its grip. This was all so new to her. So wonderful, so free, so totally uninhibited that she was terrified of losing it. Terrified of the cold force of reality coming crashing down on her and making her think.

She didn't want to think. All she wanted to do was feel. Being with Ramón, kissing Ramón, caressing Ramón made her feel so perfectly out of control that she never, ever wanted to know what restraint felt like again.

'No,' she muttered again, stilling his protests with a kiss, crushing them back down his throat. 'No, not there. Here. Right here. Right now. I want you Ramón.'

'Oh, *Dios.*' It was a sigh of surrender. 'And I want you!'

Rolling onto his back, he took her with him, the strength of his arms pulling her up until she was lying over him, cushioned from the hardness of the floor by the strength of his body. She had barely registered his intent before his hands were on her thighs, tugging her legs apart so that she straddled him, feeling the hot power of him probing the central core of her.

'Ra—' she began, but choked the word off as his mouth fastened on her breast, suckling and tugging at the nipple while his hands stroked her intimately, making her gasp out loud in delight. She closed her eyes to enjoy the sensation, then opened them again just as quickly, needing to look into his dark, tense face, seeing the colour scored along his cheekbones, the glaze of passion in his eyes.

'I want you,' he said again, his voice rough and raw with need. 'Want you!'

In the same moment, he shifted his hips and thrust upwards and into her, filling her completely.

Estrella's eyes opened wide, but she was no longer seeing anything. All she was aware of was her body and this man's and the point at which they were so intimately joined. The pulse of pleasure was out of control now, taking them both out of the world and into a dark, burning place where nothing mattered but each other and the burning pleasure that sent passion spiralling along every nerve in their bodies.

Sensation piled on sensation, taking them faster and faster, and higher and higher, further and further until there was nowhere to go but over the edge and into the brilliant oblivion of release.

CHAPTER SIX

SHE didn't want the morning to come.

That was the one thought in Estrella's mind whenever she woke, briefly, from the exhausted sleep into which she had sunk some time in the middle of the night. Before that Ramón had taken her from the living room and led her upstairs to his bedroom, laying her gently on the huge double bed. She had lost count of the number of times they had made love in the end, only knowing that, while her body finally gave in to satiation and weariness, her mind was still so much more than hungry.

She wanted more. Longed for, dreamed of more. Even when she was so worn out that she could barely move, but lay limp and drained in the softness of the big bed, her imagination kept throwing up wild images of the long, passionately erotic night and making her wish she had the energy to repeat the whole experience over again.

It had never been like this before. Nothing like this with Carlos, and Carlos had been her one and only lover. She didn't want to think about Carlos but she couldn't stop the memories surfacing. Because in one short night Ramón had totally obliterated everything that Carlos had taught her about lovemaking.

Or, rather everything he had not taught her. Because with Carlos she had known little or no satisfaction or pleasure. Nothing like this firestorm of sensation; this totally out-of-mind and almost out-of-body experience.

But she had always believed that she was in love with Carlos. The thought of love had never entered her head with

Ramón. And yet Ramón had taken possession of her, body and soul, driving the bitter memories of the other man's deception out of her mind. Already she found it impossible to remember him clearly. The only thing she could see if she closed her eyes was Ramón's dark, intent face above her, the molten silver of his eyes as he took possession of her again and again.

'Well, you really are going to have trouble explaining this to your *papá*.'

The low, husky voice, touched with a note of irony, jolted her out of her thoughts and back into the world. Her eyes snapped open and she turned her head to see that Ramón had come silently into the room and was standing by the door, a couple of coffee mugs in his hands.

His still-damp hair and the freshness of his skin told its own story—he was obviously newly showered and shaved. He was not just dressed but dressed in full business uniform. Another of those wonderfully tailored suits, complete with shirt and tie—blue, this time—and polished black leather shoes. All making the statement that today was all about work and definitely nothing to do with play.

'Or did you tell him you were going to spend the night with this friend of yours?'

'I—I told him to expect me when he saw me,' Estrella managed, suddenly painfully aware of the possible interpretations that he might put on her answer.

Tell him yes, she'd told her father she might be out all night, and he could easily jump to the conclusion that she had planned what had happened. That she had arrived with the intention of seducing him and ending up in his bed. Tell him no, she hadn't planned on staying, and it looked as if she was an easy conquest, falling into his hands and his bed like a ripe peach, more than ready for plucking.

'But I expect I'd better think about getting home before he phones Carmen and asks any awkward questions.'

'Drink your coffee first.' Ramón held out the mug.

It was as she hoisted herself up onto the pillows, the sheets slipping down from her body with the movement, that Estrella became painfully aware of the fact that she was totally naked under the fine Egyptian cotton. Naked, and marked with the signs of Ramón's ardent passion, she realised as she saw the faint red marks on her skin, the spots where, later in the night, the rough growth of stubble had rubbed against her shoulders and her breasts.

Fiery colour washing over her, she yanked the white sheet up higher, tucking it under her arms and almost around her neck so that she was covered from view.

'Bit late for that, isn't it?' Ramón remarked dryly, watching as she almost snatched at the mug, then moving to hook a chair forward with one foot and lowering his long body into it. 'Last night told me all I wanted about the way you look out of your clothes.'

'I wanted to make sure I didn't spill any coffee on me,' Estrella snapped, knowing she sounded unnecessarily defensive and not really caring.

His beautiful mouth twitched slightly, betraying the feelings that were carefully smoothed out from his bland response.

'Very sensible. You wouldn't want to burn that delicate skin.'

Estrella winced inside at the mockery that was behind his words. Yes, it was too late for modesty. Yes, he had seen, and touched—and more—every last inch of her body on many occasions throughout the night. But that had been last night, in the heated darkness of this bed. This morning, in the cold light of day, was quite another matter.

And the worst part of it was Ramón's own behaviour.

When she had drifted asleep last night, curled up tight against this man's lean, hard body, legs and arms intimately entwined, she had felt relaxed and at ease. She had no idea what was going to happen. Ramón had given her no answer to her rashly impulsive proposal, and until he did she had no way of knowing what the future might hold. But after a night such as the one they had just shared, after the mutual passion and pleasure they'd enjoyed, she had little doubt that something could be worked out. She had been far too tired to talk about things then, but in the morning would do.

But the morning she had anticipated had begun with her waking with her body still tangled up with Ramón's. She had imagined a long, leisurely surfacing, slowly shaking off the clinging shreds of sleep. They might even—more likely than not—make love again. And in the relaxed and comfortable aftermath of that new passion, with Ramón's arms round her, her head on his chest, then surely they would be able to talk.

That Ramón she would have been able to reason with. More, she would be able to open her heart and tell him everything. Tell him the whole painful truth about Carlos and about her past. But this Ramón was a very different matter.

Did he know what message his actions communicated? That when she had been anticipating waking together, lingering in bed together, talking together, loving, then his behaviour in not just getting up, but showering and getting dressed spoke only too eloquently of his need to put as much distance as he could between them. He didn't have to say anything. His physical appearance, just sitting there, communicated everything perfectly without the use of any words.

Their night together was over. His day had begun. Ramón

Dario, media executive, was up and dressed and ready to start work. And she…

She could what?

What did he expect her to do? Get up, shower and dress like him and then—leave?

But what about last night? What about everything that had happened between them?

'You're going to work.'

Stupid and inane as it was, it was all that she could manage.

'Obviously.'

Ramón's tone was giving nothing away, and his expression, his eyes, revealed even less. His face was a blank, impenetrable mask and heavy lids hooded his eyes, hiding them from her.

'But why?'

It was the wrong thing to say. She knew that as soon as she saw his head go back, his eyes narrowing sharply.

'It's what I do. The company won't run itself.'

'But I would have thought that today…'

She was just making matters worse with every word she spoke. Now a dark frown drew Ramón's black brows together sharply and she could feel the rejection that radiated from him as if it were a physical force.

'And what,' he said, icily cold, 'what makes today any different from the rest of my life?'

'Well—I would have expected…'

'You'd have expected?' Ramón echoed dangerously when she hesitated, the thoughts tangling up inside her head so that she was incapable of words.

'That you—that I…'

'Are you still thinking about this crazy idea that we might marry?' Ramón demanded harshly. 'Because if you are then I suggest you forget it straight away. There isn't going to be any wedding of convenience between us. I told your father that.'

'But last night—it wasn't my father who asked—I proposed…'

'And I'm giving you the same answer that I gave your father.'

The words came laced with an icy venom that made Estrella shrink back against her pillows, clutching the mug until the knuckles on her fingers turned white.

'I'm not looking for marriage. I don't want marriage; I never have. I like my life just the way it is. And if I ever did take a wife, then it would be someone I had chosen for myself. Not someone who offers themselves on a plate for a price—even the price of a television company.'

She looked stunned, Ramón reflected cynically. She actually looked stunned. She really couldn't have believed that he would go through with her impossible scheme. If there had ever been such a scheme in the first place.

He'd been taken off guard last night. Unprepared for the way that she had kissed him, he had been completely off balance in seconds, as hot and horny as any teenager. And he didn't regret a moment of it. Except that now it seemed that last night's pleasure came with a kickback in the form of Estrella believing that he had agreed to go along with her crazy plan.

'But—but last night…'

'Last night? You're not trying to make out there was anything special about last night? You wanted me. I wanted you—I gave you what you wanted.'

'And took what you wanted too.'

'Yeah, and why not? You were the one making all the moves.'

Though he had to admit that the way she looked now, in his bed, with her eyes still blurry with sleep, jet-black hair spread out on the pillows and her golden skin in glowing contrast to the pure white of the sheets, he was severely tempted to make a few moves of his own. The instant hardening of his body when he had come into the room and seen her lying there, warm and relaxed, her eyes closed, had been almost too much temptation to take. But this was the morning, and he had had a long time to think over the foolishness of last night and realise that it had to stop.

He of all people knew just how destructive it could be to tie yourself in marriage to a woman who didn't love you. Hadn't his own mother done that with Reuben—and hadn't both of them lived to regret it desperately? Just the thought of finding out, at some point in the future, that a child he wanted wasn't his made his guts tie themselves into knots.

It was going no further. No matter what Estrella might think or hope for.

It had to end now. For good. He had to make sure that she left and never came back. Because if she did, he might not have the sense or the strength to do this again.

Ramón drained what was left of his coffee and deposited the empty mug on the floor.

'You threw yourself at me and I'm a normal, red-blooded male. What the hell did you think I was going to do? Say, Sorry, dear, but I'm not in the mood, and walk away?'

'You—you did once. At the castle.'

Yes, he had, and it had damn near killed him. He hadn't been about to go through that again too willingly. The withdrawal symptoms that his aroused body had suffered had been his personal idea of hell.

'But that was when you said that you wouldn't let me touch you if I was the last man on earth. Last night you were in a very different mood altogether.'

'I—I thought...'

'You thought what, sweetheart? You surely didn't have some crazy idea that I'd fallen in love with you?'

That seemed to appall her as much as it did him.

'What? No! No way! Never!'

'Good—I'm glad that your fantasy scenario doesn't go quite that far. Where are you going?'

She had dumped her own mug on the bedside cabinet and was half out of the bed, the sheet wrapped round her and trailing in her wake like a white wave.

'I'm looking for my clothes. I want to get dressed.'

She looked round the room in obvious dismay, biting her lip in concern.

'Where are my clothes? Damn you, Ramón, what have you done—?'

'Calm down!'

He held up a hand to quieten her.

'I haven't done anything with them. If you recall last night we—got rather carried away downstairs first of all. Your clothes are still in the living room. I'll go and fetch them.'

It had been the sight of her clothes—and his—scattered about the floor that had brought him to his senses, he recalled as he made his way down the stairs to the living room. The visible evidence of the way that he had let his passions rule his head, becoming a prey to his physical needs instead of thinking about the repercussions, had made his blood run cold.

How could he have been so damn stupid—and with Estrella Medrano of all people?

He had known what her personal agenda was and yet he had still jumped in blindly. She was after marriage and marriage wasn't for him. It never would be.

The clothes he had picked up and folded carefully lay in

a neat pile on the big leather armchair. The armchair on which she had been perched when she had first kissed him.

His eyes closed briefly, his blood throbbing as he remembered that kiss and what it had led to.

If he'd had any sense he would have stopped it right then and there. But from the moment her lips had touched his, any sense he had possessed had flown right out of the window.

He had never wanted any woman with half the intensity that he had wanted Estrella last night.

He still wanted her, *maldito sea!*

Bending to pick up the bundle of clothes, he stopped abruptly, stilled by the sight of the scraps of peach-coloured satin and lace he had taken from her willing body only a few hours before. Just for a moment he touched them, resting his fingers very lightly on the silky material, and instantly wished that he hadn't.

In the space of a jerking heartbeat, his mind was filled with wild, erotic images. Memories of how it had felt last night to kiss Estrella's soft, sweetly perfumed skin, to cup and weigh the warm softness of her breasts in both his hands, to feel the hardened nipples peaking against his palms.

His clouded eyes went to the spot on the floor where he had lain. Where he had pulled her on top of him and...

'*Infierno,* no!'

He had to stop this or he would never be able to hold out against her. Right now all he could think of was going back upstairs and into the bedroom where he had left Estrella. He wanted to grab hold of her, rip the white, enveloping sheet from her slender body and throw her on the bed. He wanted to bury himself in her soft and welcoming heat and...

And he must not.

She wanted marriage, and he was not prepared to offer

her that commitment, not even for the financial incentive she offered. He was not going to be bought, either by her or her father.

Marriage was supposed to be for ever. A lifetime commitment. If even his own mother couldn't stay faithful to her marriage vows, then how could he expect that any woman might? Especially one who only wanted him for her own reasons—none of which was love.

Turning his eyes away from the provocative temptation of the slivers of peach satin, he dumped the tee shirt on top of them and set off upstairs again.

Estrella was just where he had left her, standing by the window, with the white sheet wrapped around her. He had hoped that she might find his robe or something else that she could at least pull on. Anything that would do a more effective job of concealing those feminine curves, the swell of her breasts against the fine fabric.

The sheet was wrapped so tightly around her that it outlined every female inch of her, and the tumble of her tousled black hair over her naked shoulders only added fuel to the fire of temptation that his thoughts downstairs had already set raging inside him.

But one look into her stony, set face, seeing the stormy rejection that flared in her eyes, was almost enough to douse the flames in a single moment. Almost—not quite. But she looked so unwelcoming and unapproachable that he had no difficulty in staying on the opposite side of the bed, depositing her clothes on the crumpled covers with a faint mocking bow.

'Your clothes, señorita.'

'Thank you.'

It was offered with obvious reluctance, almost forced from her lips.

'And now, if you don't mind, I'd prefer to have some privacy while I get dressed.'

There was something in her voice, a disturbing quaver that made him pause in the act of turning away. Was it possible? Could it be tears that made her eyes glisten even more than usual?

'Estrella...' he began, but she shook her head fiercely so that the black hair flew in a wild halo round her head.

'I don't want to hear a word from you—not another word! Now get out and leave me alone!'

'Fine.'

It was curt and clipped and absolutely cold.

'I'll wait for you downstairs.'

'You do that.'

She waited pointedly, hands on her hips, until he had left the room and she heard his footsteps descending the stairs. Only then did she disentangle herself from the sheet and head for the *en suite* bathroom.

She had no idea how long she stayed under the cascade of hot, hot water. She only knew that, no matter how many times she scrubbed her skin, she still couldn't find a way to feel clean.

What had she done?

Her thoughts winced away from the memory of last night and the way that she had—in Ramón's own words—thrown herself at him.

'Oh, how could I?'

She spoke the words aloud, shaking her head in despair at the thought of her own foolishness.

'How could I?'

Last night, asking Ramón to marry her had seemed like a good idea. It had seemed the only way out, to free herself from her father's constant anger, the nagging, the bullying that had been her life ever since she had messed up so badly with Carlos.

Carlos.

There it was again, that sudden, unnerving realisation of how very differently she had behaved with Carlos from the way she was with Ramón.

Carlos had made it very plain from the start that he wanted her in his bed, but, never having slept with a man, and nervous for her reputation in the small, old-fashioned Spanish community, she had held back as long as she'd dared. She had never even known, never suspected that he was married. Until it was too late.

But with Ramón she hadn't even thought, let alone had any time for second thoughts. One touch, one kiss from him and she had gone up in flames. She had been on fire all through the night, burning up with passion. So now it seemed fitting that everything lay in ashes around her.

Shutting off the shower reluctantly, she dressed in the tee shirt and jeans of yesterday, carefully blanking off her mind so that she didn't have to think, as she put them on, of the way that Ramón had taken them off her last night. She wished she had had some cosmetics other than the mascara and a light lip gloss that were all she carried with her in her handbag. Her face looked colourless and wan without anything. She tried pinching her cheeks hard to bring a little colour into them, only to find that it faded away in the space of a couple of seconds.

Eventually she made her way downstairs, praying that Ramón might have got tired of waiting and left for his office.

In that she was disappointed. He was still in the kitchen, a pile of mail on the table at which he sat. He had made himself another mug of coffee, but was clearly not really drinking it, just as he was clearly not properly reading the letter he held in his hand.

'I'll be on my way, then,' Estrella said stiffly from the doorway.

It was the only thing she could think of to say. She had no experience of anything like this. Had never even stayed over at a man's home before, so she had no idea what the normal procedure was.

And then, of course, this particular situation could hardly be defined as normal.

Ramón's dark head snapped up and he focused cloudy grey eyes on her pale face.

'Don't go yet. You haven't eaten a thing. Wouldn't you like some breakfast?'

'I think it would choke me,' Estrella tossed out, hating the way that he was playing the role of the polite and considerate host when the situation demanded nothing of the sort.

'I'm not that bad a cook.' Ramón offered a smile, which she stubbornly refused to respond to even though it was a struggle. 'And we never did get that meal last night.'

'No, we didn't.'

If only she'd accepted his offer of food, then she might not have acted quite so stupidly. She might have kept her head. Oh, how she wished she had!

'But I still don't want anything to eat. I just want to get home.'

'Estrella—'

Ramón pushed back his chair and stood up, disturbingly tall and powerful in the confines of the kitchen.

'The situation at home—is it really that bad?'

Estrella eyed him warily, wondering just where he was heading now.

'You've seen my father,' was all she said.

'Then why don't you leave? Get a job—'

He broke off abruptly when she couldn't hold back the cynical laugh that showed her feelings.

'You have to be joking! I repeat—you've seen my father. He's a couple of generations older than any of my contemporaries' parents—older than yours, I'll bet! But mentally he's older than that again. And I'm his only child—the Medrano heiress. My upbringing was positively mediaeval. I have no skills, no training.'

And after the truth about Carlos had come out, she had had a near complete breakdown. She hadn't been able to think or act. Her father had moved in then and taken over her life and he'd been running it ever since.

'No one would offer me a job.'

'I would.'

'What?'

She couldn't believe what she was hearing.

'I'll give you a job—in the Alcolar Corporation. You could leave home—get a flat somewhere.'

'You'd do that?'

He thought she was offering him a compliment. She could see that from the light in his eyes, the sudden, quick, devastating smile.

'I would.'

'You think I'm worth employing, but not worth marrying?'

'That isn't what I said, damn it!'

'And I don't recall ever saying that I wanted a job!'

To be employed by him would just be too much. She would have to see him, speak to him, and every time she did she would remember last night and the humiliation that had greeted her this morning.

'I wouldn't touch your job if it came gift-wrapped in pure gold. I don't want anything from you!'

'You did last night.'

The dangerous, dark undertone was back in his voice.

'Last night was different.'

'Yeah, last night you thought you were going to get what you wanted from me.'

Ramón had finally lost his grip on the temper he had been reining in. He'd tried to help her and she'd thrown it back in his face. 'But I have this strong aversion to being used,' he snarled viciously, and watched her head go back, her eyes opening wide.

'You weren't being used!' Estrella protested.

'No? Believe me, sweetheart, that's what it felt like.'

'Oh, so now it's using you to offer you what you said you wanted most in all the world.'

For a moment he thought she'd meant herself in his bed and his head spun with shock to think that she knew. A moment later his thought processes cleared and he realised she meant the television company. The television company that, disturbingly, hadn't been the first thing to come into his mind.

'I told you, the price on that was way too high.'

'You didn't seem to think so last night.'

'Last night was just sex! I never offered any promises.'

He'd hit home with that. He saw her blink hard, withdraw just for a moment. But when she came back at him she had clearly just been taking time to prepare her attack.

'Then it's just as well you didn't, because last night I might have been fool enough to accept them. This morning I'm thinking straight again and I have to say I'm inclined to agree with you about that price. Like you, it's not one I'm prepared to pay.'

'Of course not, because, as your father was at great pains to point out to me, I don't exactly have the respectable Catalan lineage that he was hoping for.'

'No—that's why you came tenth in the list of possible suitors.'

That stung. It was like the flick of a whip on his male pride and it drove him to push aside all consideration of fairness or restraint. The other Estrella was back—the hard, calculating woman he detested. And he needed that reminder. He'd come close to swallowing her hard-luck story.

'So why did you throw yourself at me last night?'

Her chin came up, deep brown eyes flashing fiercely.

'Isn't it obvious? I was just hot for you.'

'What? You wanted a bit of rough? Is that how you get your kicks, lady? Do you enjoy slumming it? Is that what your relationship with Carlos Perea was all about?'

'Leave Car—leave him out of this!'

'Oh, okay, I'll do that. For now. But tell me, my lovely Doña Medrano—*querida*...'

Ramón laced the words with an acid that was aimed to sting every bit as much as her earlier comment.

'Of those other nine suitors of yours—how many of them did you throw yourself at as you did with me last night? Did you try them all out—a test run, so to speak, to see if they came up to your demanding standards? Did you—?'

The crack of her hand hitting the side of his face silenced him more effectively than the actual slap and for a moment they froze and just stared at each other, Estrella wide-eyed with shock at her own actions, her breathing frantic and rawly uneven.

'Well, I guess I asked for that,' Ramón admitted, refusing even to rub at his stinging cheek.

'You did!'

Both her arms came up in a wild, uncontrolled gesture, crossing in front of her face in a way that was both furious and yet at the same time strangely defensive.

'I had nothing to do with those others—nothing! If you

must know, you are the only one of them that I ever spoke to properly, the only one I ever kissed—the only one I ever—ever…'

She choked to a halt, obviously unable to complete the sentence.

'And is that supposed to make me feel honoured?'

Estrella shook her head furiously, her long hair flying around her face in a wild black cloud.

'Not at all. If it does anything—it just goes to show, after you and Carlos, what an appalling, stupid, naïve judge of men I really am!'

'I—' Ramón began, but she cut him off before he had a chance to say anything more.

'Not a word!' she spat at him. 'Not a single word! I've heard all I ever want to from you for the rest of my life. You'd have thought I'd learn my lesson after coming up against a user and manipulator the first time, but, no, obviously I'm so damn stupid, I really need my nose rubbing in things! Well, you've done that for me, Señor Dario—and I thank you for your instructions. This time I really think I've got it—I've learned my lesson once and for all. And I don't think I'm ever likely to forget.'

And before Ramón could gather his scatted thoughts to answer her she had whirled on her heel, snatching up her bag, and fled, letting the door slam behind her.

CHAPTER SEVEN

'Just what is wrong with you these days, Ramón? You're wandering round in a dream.'

'Perhaps he's in love. Is that right, Ramón? Is the great Señor ''marriage is not for me'' Dario actually smitten at last?'

'Don't tease, Mercedes.'

It was Cassie who spoke, earning herself a quick, grateful smile from her brother-in-law. 'I just think Ramón has a lot on his mind.'

'A lot of woman!' Ramón's sister laughed. 'Is that it? It would have to be someone really special to knock my brother sideways like this!'

A lot of woman. He certainly knew someone who fitted that description, Ramón reflected. And it was true that she had hardly ever been out of his mind in the week since she had stormed out of his apartment and out of his life.

He had tried to stop her. He had gone after her almost at once, but those few seconds' hesitation had been all she'd needed. Fate had been on her side, it seemed. She must have stepped into a lift as soon as she'd left the apartment, achieved the impossible by getting a taxi the minute she'd walked out onto the street, and by the time he'd got outside she had gone. She had vanished and it was as if she had never existed.

'You're not still brooding over that Medrano deal?'

It was his father who spoke. Juan Alcolar was leaning back in his chair, apparently relaxed, a glass of the finest red wine from his son's vineyard in his hands. But his eyes were sharp and assessing as they rested on his son's face.

'In a way—yes,' Ramón admitted reluctantly, knowing that the problem was nothing at all to do with the deal, but everything to do with the Medrano daughter. Even just to hear her surname spoken aloud made his nerves tighten, his jaw tensing.

'I told you to forget about that,' his father told him. 'Medrano's a narrow-minded old goat. He always was too proud of his Catalan heritage for his own good. Too set in his ways too.'

'Says the man who forgets that we have Andalusian blood in our veins as well as Catalan,' commented Joaquin, wandering into the room and dropping an affectionate kiss on the top of Cassie's blonde head. 'You and Medrano are as bad as each other, *papá*. You can't ignore Great-grandfather, no matter how you might want to.'

A couple of weeks ago, this conversation would have been unlikely, to say the least, Ramón reflected. But since Joaquin and Cassie had announced they were getting married—adding the extra good news that Juan's second grandchild was on the way—a new warmth had developed between the older man and his first-born son. For the first time in years they seemed relaxed with each other.

Joaquin had mellowed too. Watching him now with his arm around his fiancée, no one would ever have believed that less than a month ago they had been on the point of splitting up completely. Had split up, in fact. Cassie had even ended up living with Ramón for a while.

But all that was behind them now. All they'd needed was to really talk to each other—and for Joaquin to forget his crazy idea that he wasn't made for a lasting relationship.

A sudden memory of his own voice declaring, 'I don't

want marriage; I never have,' made him restless, moving to refill his coffee-cup from a pot on the sideboard.

'And you're not much better,' he told his older half-brother now. 'When it comes to stubbornness and pride, it seems to me that the Alcolar men are just about equal.'

'Pots and kettles,' Cassie murmured laughingly, looking up from the list of wedding invitations she was compiling.

'What?'

Ramón frowned his lack of comprehension.

'In England we have a saying about the pot calling the kettle black—which means they're both equally guilty. I think that applies to you as well as Joaquin.'

'And you are every bit as much of an Alcolar as Joaquin,' Mercedes put in. 'When it comes to stubbornness and pride then you two are just as bad as each other.'

'I—' Ramón began protestingly, but then his voice failed him as he recalled the number of times that he had picked up a phone to call the Castillo Medrano and then put it down again.

He had even set out for Estrella's home once, but had turned the car around after a couple of miles.

Deciding that discretion was the best policy here, he said nothing and drank his coffee instead.

'Pots and kettles,' Cassie murmured, her mouth quirking up at the corner.

The phrase stayed with him all the way home. It was in his head as he fell asleep. It was there when he woke up in the morning.

But it was the time in between that told him exactly why it was there.

His sleep, such as it was, had been filled with dreams. And the dreams had been filled with just one person.

Estrella Medrano.

The wild, heated, erotic images of her that had played

across his mind had plagued his night, making him toss and turn uneasily until he had finally woken, bathed in sweat and caught up in a strangling tangle of sheets. And even in the morning when he woke they were still there, tormenting him with memories, reproaching him for losing his temper so badly, making him restless and ill at ease so that he couldn't concentrate on anything.

If he closed his eyes he saw her face. If he sat at his desk he was sure that he could scent her perfume on the air, feel the silken slide of her long black hair against his face. And once, when he answered the phone and heard a woman's voice, he was sure that it was her on the other end of the line.

But it was only Mercedes, ringing up to tell him about a trip to England she was planning. For perhaps the first time ever he couldn't bring himself to give his younger sister the indulgent attention he usually showed her and he could tell that she was annoyed and upset when she finally hung up the phone.

Just what the hell was wrong with him? Ramón asked himself, picking up a file and trying to remember what he was supposed to be doing with it.

Did he really have to ask that question? Didn't he know already just what the answer would be? The two words that summed up everything that was preying on his mind, driving him to distraction.

Estrella Medrano.

The conversation they had had that night in his flat played over and over in his head until he felt that he was going insane.

'You want me to marry you?'

'Yes. Yes, I do.'

'Why me?'

'Because you weren't going to ask me when my father wanted you to. You walked out on the deal you wanted...'

'And this...'

The memory of just what 'this' had meant made his body clench his blood heat, his pulse run wild.

He'd told himself to let her go. To forget her. Who was he trying to kid?

He couldn't forget her. He wanted her.

He wanted her so badly that it hurt.

'And is there nothing else that would give you the same satisfaction?'

'Nothing else that matches it.'

Another snatch of conversation from the night he had spent with Estrella floated into his mind, making him shake his head in despair at himself. He had thought that the deal with her father was what mattered to him. He had wanted that deal, had planned, schemed, negotiated, worked his butt off to get that deal.

Only now did he see that it came in second place, if that. A long, long way second.

He'd wanted the deal. He'd wanted the television station—he still did. Wanted them so much.

But he wanted Estrella Medrano so much more.

'Infierno!'

In a fury of restlessness he tossed down his pen and stood up, yanking his jacket from where it hung on the back of his chair. If he kept this up he would go completely insane!

He was just going to see her, he told himself. Just see her and talk to her and...

His mind wouldn't go beyond that point.

He didn't know what was beyond that point. The real question didn't dawn on him until he was in his car, with the engine running.

He wasn't really thinking of marrying Estrella Medrano after all—was he?

Estrella's head was aching brutally. She had hardly slept all week, and tonight was positively the last straw. When her father had announced that they were expecting a guest for dinner, she had actually taken a few minutes to register quite what he meant.

But then she had seen the look in his eyes, the harsh set to his mouth, and she had known.

It was not just any casual visitor, not some friend of her father making a social call. He had found another possible suitor for her.

'*Papá*—please don't do this...'

It was some time since she had tried to fight. But after the humiliation and the embarrassment she had endured with Ramón Dario, she knew she had to try. She just couldn't go through it all again.

Her arguments, her pleading fell on deaf ears. Alfredo was totally determined, and nothing she could do would sway or change his mind.

'If you hadn't dragged the Medrano name in the dust, playing around with a married man, ruining a fine woman's life—not to mention those two poor children—then you wouldn't be in this situation. But I warn you, my girl, I'm coming to the end of my patience.'

He came very close, glaring into her face, his hand coming up to emphasise the point so ferociously that Estrella shrank back fearfully.

'You do something to sort your life out and fast or you'll find yourself out on the streets where you belong.'

'*Papá*...'

'No. No arguments,' Alfredo spat at her. 'I'm telling you—either you make a decent marriage or you're out of here with just the clothes you have on your back. You'll take nothing else with you—and you can sink or swim, it won't matter to me.'

She could have no doubt at all that he meant it, Estrella reflected. For weeks now, Alfredo's temper had been growing more and more uncertain, his moods darker and more dangerous. She'd been terribly afraid of what he might do next. Now she knew.

Suddenly Ramón's offer of a job didn't seem quite so unappealing. But if she took him up on that offer, she would have to crawl back to him, beg him to let her have the favour she had so foolishly tossed back in his face.

More than the offer, she told herself. Recalling the way she had slapped him, she knew that she'd killed her chances then and there, without a hope of rescue or reconciliation. The offer of a job wouldn't be available any more. Ramón was far more likely to join with her father in slamming the door shut in her face and not caring a damn about what happened to her after that.

Deciding that for now discretion was the better part of valour, she went along with her father's orders, on the surface at least. She prepared for the dinner ahead of her, dressing in the rich blue silk dress as he had instructed, fixing her make-up, even piling her hair up high on the top of her head with a couple of ornate combs. All the time her stomach was heaving nauseously, fear twisting in every nerve as she faced the prospect, not of the proposal her father thought he had bought and paid for, but of the inevitable confrontation with Alfredo afterwards.

The mood he was in, it was going to be appalling.

It was worse than she had anticipated. Esteban Ramirez, the suitor who had been selected for her this time, was a man who was old enough to be her father. He was also heavily overweight, with lank, greasy hair and an unpleasant body odour problem. But that didn't stop him from eyeing her up and down like a prize beast at an auction. He also took every opportunity to brush up close to her or to touch her, patting or pawing her with his hot, moist hands every time she was near to him.

'You are a lovely young thing,' he said, practically drooling as he took her in to dinner. 'Lovely. I'm sure we're going to get on so well together.'

The meal was an ordeal by food. Estrella was incapable of eating anything, merely pushing things round on her plate, finally lifting something to her mouth, but knowing that, as just the smell of the chicken was enough to make her gag, she would never be able to swallow it. Hastily she lowered her fork again and reached for the glass of wine.

But even that conspired against her. By some malign coincidence, the drink that her father had selected was the same rich, ruby wine that Ramón had served her the week before in his apartment. Just one sip of it brought back such a rush of memories that her throat closed up instantly and she had to force herself to swallow in order not to choke painfully.

'Is something the matter?' her father demanded sharply, noting her uncomfortable expression.

'No,' Estrella managed to gasp. 'Nothing—I—I'm fine!'

But fine was the exact opposite of the way she was feeling. The taste of the wine had revived all the burning, erotic dreams that had haunted the little sleep she had had over the past week, throwing up images of Ramón's long, lean body, the dark silk of his hair. She could feel again his touch, his kisses, taste his mouth on hers as she tried to moisten her parched lips.

She could hear his deep, husky voice in her thoughts.

'You want me to marry you?'

'Why me?'

And there too were her own foolish, unthinking words.

'And this… And this… And this…'

'What—who did you say?'

Her father's voice. She had been so adrift on her memories that she hadn't been aware of one of the servants coming to Alfredo and whispering in his ear.

'Who?'

Alfredo shot her a coldly assessing glance, one that tugged every already taut muscle even tighter, twisted the nerves in her stomach until she gasped in pain.

'Dario?'

For a second she thought that she had heard wrong. She had to have heard wrong. But then her father turned to her.

'It seems that Ramón Dario has come to see you. Do you know why?'

Estrella opened her mouth but nothing would come out. Nothing but a weak, unintelligible croak that meant nothing at all.

It wasn't possible. Ramón couldn't be here. He just couldn't. To her whirling mind it felt almost as if she had conjured him up in her thoughts, making him appear because of the power of her memories. She could only shake her head as Alfredo glared at her.

'Well, I suppose we'd better see what he wants. Tell Señor Dario to come in.'

Even then, Estrella wasn't convinced that it was true. Any moment now, she told herself, Rafael would come back and say it had all been a mistake. Or she would have heard the name completely wrong and he would bring in someone else entirely…

But then Rafael returned and behind him strode the tall dark man who had been in almost her every thought, waking and sleeping, since the day he had first appeared in her life.

He was dressed much more casually than she had ever

seen him. A soft blue polo shirt flattered the hard lines of his shoulders and chest while a pair of denim jeans hugged the length of his legs, the narrow hips and lean waist, outlining every muscle with a tightness that made her throat dry.

If he was surprised to find them at dinner—and with Ramirez there as their guest—then he didn't show it. Those silvery eyes went straight to where she sat at the far side of the table, meeting her own troubled chocolate brown ones in a look that was both recognition and a challenge all in one moment. His gaze swept round the table, resting for a moment on Alfredo, a second longer on Ramirez, and she saw his eyes narrow swiftly before they returned to Estrella's father.

'Señor Medrano.'

Ramón's swift, polite smile looked the epitome of courtesy, faultless in its restraint, the way that it embraced them all. Only someone as supremely sensitive to everything about him as Estrella would have noticed the way that it was not quite natural, the momentary hesitation before he switched it on, the speed with which it faded as soon as he could. Underneath it was a coldly controlled degree of distance that hardened his jaw line, tightened the muscles of his face and turned the stormy eyes to slivers of freezing grey ice.

'Estrella…'

Ramón worked hard on controlling his voice and his expression though he was having to struggle to squash down the disgust and the anger that rose up inside him as he assessed the situation in the huge, impersonal dining room.

It didn't take a genius to work out just what was going on. He had taken in the situation in a single, searching glance around the room, and if he'd needed any help then the look on Estrella's face told its own story to anyone with

eyes to see. Right now, Ramón felt that he could read her
like a book.

She was dressed in a simple but elegant deep blue silk
dress with a halter neck, and her hair was put up in some
complicated, elaborate style that made his fingers itch to pull
out the silvery combs that held the black strands in place.
Her eyes dominated her face, deep, dark, clouded pools,
fringed by impossibly long and dark lashes. But the extra
make-up she wore, the careful shading and colouring,
couldn't disguise the shadows that lay just above the high,
slanting cheekbones, the lines of stress that tightened the
soft, luscious mouth.

She looked stunning, more beautiful than he had ever
seen her. But she also looked lost, afraid and intensely, devastatingly vulnerable. And that vulnerability appealed to everything that was male and protective in him.

She would rather be anywhere but here. That much was
plain. And the reason for her distress was easy to find. He
was the squat, fat, toadlike creature sitting opposite her at
the dining table. The one man who wasn't interested in the
interruption to the meal because he was too busy undressing
Estrella with his cold, piggy eyes.

Another man her father was trying to sell her to.

Suitor number eleven, unless he was very much mistaken.

But not for long, he promised himself. And the promise
was enough to help him rein in the temper that was threat-
ening to erupt inside him, like red hot lava boiling up inside
an active volcano.

'What can we do for you, Señor Dario?'

Her father was making it plain that he was none too happy
about being disturbed, though struggling to remember that
he needed to keep up a good front before Esteban Ramirez.
Clearly he felt that the appearance of an earlier suitor he

had tried to bribe would interfere with his plans for the
current one.

'Forgive me, Señor Medrano,' Ramón was beautifully
cool, immaculately polite. 'I had no idea that I would be
interrupting your meal like this. Estrella?'

To Estrella's total confusion he turned a reproachful
glance on her to match the note of gentle rebuke in his tone.

'You should have let me know that your father was en-
tertaining a business associate. Then I would have come
earlier—or we could have arranged to make our announcement on another occasion.'

Our announcement?

'I—'

Catching the swift, flashing glare from those grey eyes,
Estrella swallowed the exclamation of shocked astonishment
that almost escaped her, washing it back down her throat
with a hasty gulp of wine. She had no idea just what game
Ramón was playing but, until she did, she'd do better to
keep quiet and see what he was up to.

'What announcement?' Alfredo questioned sharply, his
puzzled gaze going from his daughter to the new arrival and
back again. 'Estrella?'

Estrella couldn't think of a way to answer him. Not having a tiny glimmer of an idea of what Ramón was talking
about, she didn't dare risk opening her mouth. So she just
waved her glass at the tall man standing at the other end of
the table, indicating that he should be the one to speak. She
hoped that doing so wasn't jumping from the frying-pan
right into the heart of a blazing, white-hot fire. She could
only keep quiet and pray that she could go along with whatever it was he said.

'What announcement?' Alfredo turned his attention back
to Ramón. 'What the hell is going on here?'

'Forgive me...'

Ramón put on such a good pretence of sounding genuinely apologetic that Estrella shook her head, wondering if she was hearing things—or seeing things—and it really was not Ramón who stood there. But, having blinked hard and looked again, she still saw the darkly devastating man who had stolen some part of her soul away in the moment they had first met and she had never been able to get it back since.

'I asked your daughter not to say anything until we both had time to tell you together. I had to make her promise—she wanted to say something so much earlier than this.'

Now Alfredo was looking at his daughter in evident confusion. Estrella struggled to make her expression a total blank. But inside her mind was whirling, trying to think what Ramón might be about to say—trying not to think of the things she dreaded it might be.

Recalling how furious they had both been when she had stormed out of his apartment, she shivered inside at the thought of that anger driving him to say something that would really mess up her life. Had he been angry enough for that?

'But now I see that she's kept her promise. I'm glad, because that gives me the opportunity to do this correctly. I already have Estrella's answer, but now I need yours.'

He turned towards Alfredo, suddenly stiffly formal.

'Señor Medrano, I've come here today to seek your permission to ask your daughter to marry me.'

CHAPTER EIGHT

ESTRELLA felt as if she'd been spun off the edge of the world and into a nightmare where nothing was real, everything was upside down, and she had no idea what was happening.

What was Ramón talking about?

Why was he doing this?

And, most importantly, did he mean it?

She felt as if she had lived through several lifetimes, lifetimes filled with panic and fearful uncertainty, before the world finally slowed and settled back on its axis again. In that time, Esteban Ramirez, who had clearly only been there for one reason, lost his temper and walked out in a ferocious huff, her father fired several sharp, harsh-voiced questions at Ramón—and he answered them coldly and calmly.

At least, Estrella supposed he answered them. The buzzing in her head, like the sound of a thousand alarmed bees, blurred her hearing. She felt giddy and faintly sick and it was a struggle to focus on anything. The words that Ramón had spoken circled over and over in the confusion of her thoughts.

'I've come here today to seek your permission to ask your daughter to marry me.'

He had included Estrella in his declaration, implying that she had been part of it. That she knew all about it. When she didn't know a thing about what was happening. The last time she had seen Ramón he had made it clear that he never wanted to see her again.

'Well, I'll leave you together then…'

Her father's voice seemed to come from a long, long distance away, at the end of some dark, enclosed tunnel. There was the sound of a door closing firmly and the room was quiet again.

She was alone with the silent, watchful figure of Ramón Dario.

Slowly she surfaced from the crazy nightmare world in which nothing had made sense. Blinking hard to clear her blurred gaze, she looked at the tall, dark man who stood at the bottom of the long, polished wood table, the flare of the candlelight gleaming on his burnished hair, reflected in the glitter of his eyes. She knew that he was waiting for her to speak but she could find nothing at all to say to him.

'Well, Estrella, *querida*. How does it feel to be engaged?'

'To—to who?' she managed to croak.

Her thought processes had blown a fuse, and just for the moment she had no idea at all what had happened during that discussion he had had with her father. Had he truly asked Alfredo if he could marry her?

'Why, to me, of course.'

There was laughter in his voice, but it was a cold, uncomfortable sort of sound. One that jarred on her senses and set her teeth on edge.

'Who did you think?'

She couldn't be engaged to him—it couldn't have happened, just like that—or could it?

'But why?'

'Why?' Ramón echoed, his tone superficially light but with a dangerous undernote running through it like ink trailing through water. 'I thought we'd got that perfectly clear. You get that freedom you were looking for and I get what I want.'

It was like a slap in the face.

Of course, he was only marrying her to get his hands on the television company.

It shouldn't hurt so much—realistically she had always known that. But somehow hearing it like this, spoken in cold blood, it was far more shocking than she had ever anticipated. The realisation that she, as a person, meant nothing at all to him, except as a means to an end, slashed at her soul, leaving her shivering with misery deep inside.

And what did that mean? Had she really wanted more? Had she really hoped for something else? Something with more feeling in it? Something that made this into a real marriage, based on—on…?

Based on love? The word slid into her thoughts, unwelcome and unwanted.

No! With a struggle she pushed it away. She'd thought she was in love with Carlos, and he had claimed to be in love with her. It wasn't until she had learned the truth that she had seen that there was no love in their relationship at all. He had just wanted her, and had been prepared to lie and cheat and deceive—even commit a crime to get her. Ramón had made no such pretences. He hadn't lied. In fact, quite the opposite, he had been so bluntly truthful that she could be in no doubt as to what he felt about her.

She had only herself to blame. She had offered herself on a plate to this man, for the price of the TV company, and she had no right to complain if he took up her offer on exactly the terms she had given. He didn't have more to give; didn't want more from her.

'What's the problem, Estrella?' Ramón mocked now. 'Having second thoughts about the bargain you offered? Do you think you've sold yourself too cheaply? Or perhaps you want me to get down on one knee and ask you to marry me formally?'

'No!'

Shock pushed the word from her lips. The image that flew into her brain of this proud, devastating man kneeling at her feet for something that was little more than a lie was too appalling to think of.

'No, there'll be no need for that.'

Unease made her voice colder than she had ever intended.

'But I'm sure that it was what my father had in mind when he left us alone.'

'Your father's had more than he deserves out of this already,' Ramón growled. 'From now on, it's just the two of us and no one else.'

'That suits me.'

She was shocked to think just how much it did suit her. His words had sent a rush of warmth through her body, making it glow with unexpected delight.

'But I should say of course that my father will expect me to have a ring.'

She was struggling to keep the conversation going. She didn't want to be here, at the opposite end of the room, sitting in solitary splendour like this. Just the sight of him had revived all the memories of how it had felt to be in his arms and held close, to feel the heat of his body next to hers.

Sitting here, with the space of the huge dining table between them, she felt lost and alone, shiveringly cold in spite of the warmth of the room. But she didn't know how to bridge the gap that was there between them, the mental separation far more difficult to overcome than the physical. All she had to do was to get up and take a few, just a very few, steps to reach him. But she couldn't find the mental strength to make herself do it.

'Of course. We'll choose one tomorrow—if we are going through with this.'

'And are we?'

The look he turned on her was a strange blend of cynicism and a lurking, dark thread of humour.

'Do you think your father would let me back out now that I've finally agreed to his terms?'

This had to be the most ridiculous conversation to be having immediately after becoming engaged, Ramón couldn't help reflecting. She was still sitting at the table at one end of the room, and he was here, miles away, or at least that was how it felt. If this had been anything like a real marriage, she would be in his arms now, held close, and their conversation would be punctuated by kisses, quick, ardent kisses, long, lingering, sensual kisses...

Hell, he wanted her in his arms.

'So—what made you change your mind?'

How did he answer that?

The truth was that he hadn't truly known that he'd changed it until he'd found himself on the road here. Even then, he'd told himself that he was just going to see. That he could stop, turn around at any point along the journey.

It hadn't been until he'd walked into this room and seen her sitting there that he had known. That he had felt the moment of complete, total conviction that he had to have this woman in his life, whatever it took.

'Coming in here...'

He'd started the sentence before he caught himself up, realising what he had been about to say.

'Coming in here and seeing the toad you had as your dinner companion. I take it he was suitor number eleven?'

'Yes.' Her eyes went to the chair in which Esteban Ramirez had been sitting and she gave a delicate little shudder of distaste. 'Yes, he was.'

'Then it looks as if I got here just in time. Your father would actually have sold you to him?'

Her smile was bleak, desolate and lost.

'He had a name to offer me—a respectable, married name.'

Ramón muttered something succinct and very rude and her smile grew just the tiniest bit.

'Is it really so very different between us? You could say I—s-sold myself to you for the price of the television company.'

'Hell, no—we have more between us than that!'

'We do?'

When she turned those big eyes on him, he felt as if his insides were becoming molten; nothing but heat. It was almost as if there were two totally separate Estrellas. The one who looked so fragile that he feared his touch might actually shatter her, and the harder, brittle woman he had first met, the one who had such a reputation locally. The second was the type of female he despised. A female who was so selfish that she stole another woman's husband.

Which one was the real Estrella? He couldn't begin to guess.

But in both of those women was a third Estrella. The hot-bloodedly passionate, unbelievably sexy, physically devastating Estrella Medrano whom he had discovered in one blazing night a week ago.

He would do anything to have that woman again. To have her in his arms, in his bed, in his life. That was why he was here and the damn TV company was a long, long way second.

'Like what?'

Ramón laughed again, this time with a touch of genuine warmth. He knew that that warmth must show on his face, lighting in his eyes, in his smile. He could see the response, mirrored faintly in Estrella's own face.

'Do you really have to ask me that?'

He held out his hand, long fingers beckoning slightly.

'Come here to me, Estrella. Come to me and let me show you. Let me remind you just what there is between us.'

She made a move as if to do as he said and come to him, then froze stiffly in her seat. Her eyes were huge and dark as polished ebony, fixed on his face, with a strange uncertainty taking all the colour from her cheeks.

'Estrella…' Ramón murmured huskily. 'Come.'

Still she lingered, tensed as if to move, but not moving.

With a faint frown that was more confused than angry he let his hand drop to his side again and he took several swift strides to where she sat. Those deep, dark eyes watched him come, seeming to grower wider, darker, with every second.

When he stopped by her chair, her face lifted so that her upward gaze was caught and held by his glinting silvery one, and he heard her faintly indrawn gasp of breath as he closed his hands around the tops of her arms, not hard, but holding her firmly and securely.

'You're not afraid of me?'

He couldn't iron out the faint unevenness that the question put into his voice.

'Not the Estrella who came to my apartment—who—proposed…' he let his tongue linger over the word, turning it into an almost sensual sound '…so wonderfully the other night. That Estrella was afraid of no one.'

He felt the tremor that ran through the fine bones of her body and looked down into her face even more sharply.

'That was just one night…' she managed huskily. 'Marriage is for—for—'

She swallowed down the word as if she suddenly feared expressing it.

'Marriage is different.'

'Not that different.'

Slowly he lifted her, drawing her out of her seat and

pulling her up the length of his body. The rich blue silk of her dress whispered against him and her perfume reached out to enclose him. Had she worn this for the toad—or to give herself some much-needed courage to face yet another suitor?

'You know what that one night was like…'

His voice was low and husky, rough-edged and raw.

'Imagine a lifetime of such nights—each one better than the last.'

He saw her throat move as she swallowed hard, the way a pink tongue snaked out to moisten her dry lips.

'Marriage is more than just nights.'

'But these won't be *just* nights. They will amazing, spectacular nights. Nights you will never forget. Nights you will spend your days longing for, your sleep dreaming of.'

Still she didn't look convinced. What had happened to the bold, the forward, the seductive Estrella, who had enticed his soul out of his body with just one kiss?

'And will that be enough?'

'It will be enough for me. Do you want proof? I can give you this…'

Bending his head, he took the softness of her lips in an equally soft and gentle kiss. It was a kiss that drew a sigh from her, a faint, lingering sound of pure delight. Even the very gentleness of it clutched at his senses, making his body clench in sharp demand.

'And this…'

Still gently, he deepened the kiss, easing her mouth open. Letting his tongue dance with hers. The taste of her intoxicated, the warmth of her body whispered to his, the feel of her satin skin against his cheek was pure enticement in a touch.

The heavy, honeyed throb of desire through his veins was so different from before. This time there was no harsh, hun-

gry edge to it, no screaming demand. Only heat and sweet-
ness and longing that made him wish they were anywhere
but here, in this cold and stiffly furnished, old-fashioned
room with the heavy dark furniture, the tapestried walls, the
stone-edged windows.

What this feeling needed was the warmest, softest bed
available. The smoothest sheets in the finest Egyptian cotton, the crackle and glow of a fire in the hearth... And a
long, long night ahead of them.

'Won't this be enough for anyone?' he whispered against
her cheek.

'Oh, yes,' she breathed. 'Oh, yes...'

Her eyelids seemed heavy, hard to lift, as if she were
waking from a drugged sleep, but as they fluttered open and
he looked deep into the dazed brown of her eyes he knew
that she was his. Her slender body swayed towards him,
seeming to have no will of her own to hold it upright, and
her mouth sought his again, seeking, tasting, enticing.

She was as lost in desire as he was, and right now he
asked for nothing more.

'You're mine,' it was a raw edged sound of triumph.
'Mine and only mine.'

The memory of the toad, of Esteban Ramirez sitting opposite her, his hooded eyes fixed on her lovely face, slid
into his mind, making acid rise in his throat. Just the thought
of him touching her, of his hands on Estrella's soft body,
made him grit his teeth against the rising savagery of his
anger.

'How could I ever let another man have you...?'

The words slashed into the golden haze that filled
Estrella's mind, tearing away the protection of the sensual
warmth that his kiss had stirred in her. She had welcomed
that warmth. She had needed it, longed for it. Prayed it was
still there.

But now here was this sudden change. This new note in Ramón's voice. The dangerous tone of ruthless possession that lurked in the dark undertow of his words.

'*How could I ever let another man have you…?*'

'There—there's no one…'

'No one?'

Ramón's laughter was harsh, bitter, and totally without warmth.

'What about suitor number eleven? What about him and his so-respectable name?'

'Please!' She shuddered at the thought. 'You couldn't wish that on me.'

'But your father would have.'

Was that his only reason? She couldn't help asking herself. Had he come just to take possession of her as if she were some slave, some precious item he could buy for himself if the price was right? Something he hadn't really valued until the thought that perhaps some other man might want it—that some other man might have a chance of possessing it—had made him realise how much he actually desired it for himself?

'And I would have said no. You know that. You have to know it. You are the only one…'

'Yeah, I know,' Ramón finished for her when the words deserted her suddenly. 'You're hot for me.'

For one dreadful moment she thought that he was having second thoughts. She knew that his mind had flown back to the moment in his apartment when she had flung those words at him.

'You were hot for me,' he muttered again in a savage undertone.

But then, just as she thought that she couldn't hold her breath any longer, when her sharp white teeth were mangling her bottom lip as she chewed at it in nervous dread, he suddenly looked down into her face again. To her astonishment his ruthlessly guarded face suddenly broke into a brilliant, flashing, devastating smile.

'And I for you, my star. I'm more than hot—I want you so much that I can't function. I can't work, I can't sleep. You've taken over my life and I won't be myself again until I have you in my bed. And if marriage is what it takes to get me there—then we'll marry.'

Was she really going to do this? Estrella asked herself. Was she really going through with this crazy idea of marrying someone who didn't love her—someone who only wanted her? But she had thought—had let herself believe—that Carlos had loved her. And everything he'd said had been a lie from start to finish.

Ramón at least was brutally honest with her. He wanted her—and she wanted him. Oh, how she wanted him! Even now, just standing beside him, every sense in her body was wildly alert, aching with need. Her father and his parade of suitors, the misery of her life in the castle, the gossip, all faded into insignificance beside the fulfilment she had found in Ramón's bed, the ecstasy she had known.

'We'll marry,' she echoed, her voice low, but firm.

'Soon,' Ramón put in sharply, and she could only nod her head in silent agreement.

A thought occurred to her, and she suddenly looked up into his taut, controlled face, seeing the glaze of desire in his eyes, the faint wash of colour along the carved cheekbones.

'This marriage...' she managed hesitantly, not really daring to ask herself why she said it. 'Just how long will it last?'

He didn't respond at once and she could almost see his thoughts turn inward as he considered the question, debating with himself. As she waited she fought a sharp and uncomfortable battle with her own need to know the answer, for reasons that she didn't dare to take out and look at in the cold light of day.

'Until we all get what we want,' Ramón said at last, turning steely eyes on her pale, drawn face.

'And that is?'

In her own mind, her voice gave away the sudden new importance that the question had taken on. But Ramón didn't seem to notice. Or, if he did, then nothing changed in his expression; there was no flicker of reaction in his eyes.

'You want your freedom from being assessed and examined like a prize mare at a stud farm. Your father wants a grandson to inherit the title—the Medrano land. And I...'

His voice faded, died as he looked into her face, his grey-eyed gaze centring on the curve of her mouth, the soft lips slightly parted in apprehensive uncertainty.

'And I want this...' he muttered, his tone suddenly thickening, roughening at the edges.

His dark head lowered, fast and unavoidable. His mouth closed over hers, hard, passionate and strong, his lips taking hers in a bruising kiss that had nothing of gentleness in it, but only fierce, male passion and hungry, almost savage demand.

Wordlessly, mindlessly, Estrella responded. She could do nothing else. Her body was no longer in the control of her mind; it was totally his to do as he willed with it. And what he wanted was what she wanted too.

It was a long, long time before either of them could even come apart to snatch in a much needed breath, and when they did her heart was racing so hard that her head was swimming, her eyes dazed and unfocused.

'As long as this lasts, darling,' Ramón managed, raw and uneven as her own feelings.

He kissed her again, even more passionately this time.

'As long as this lasts, we'll stay together.'

CHAPTER NINE

'THERE!'

Mercedes threaded the last of the orange blossoms into the ornate style of Estrella's black hair and stood back to admire the effect.

'I think it looks wonderful—though I say so myself. But it would help a lot if I knew just what your dress looked like.'

The look she directed at Estrella through the mirror was one of wide-eyed pleading, hoping to persuade her soon-to-be sister-in-law to let her in on the secret.

But Estrella shook her head firmly, remaining impervious to all Mercedes' wiles.

'That's my secret and mine alone. Remember, I never expected all this fuss and ceremony.'

'What?' Mercedes stared at her in frank disbelief. 'You surely never expected that Ramón would only offer you some second-rate secret marriage—or a simple, quiet event? This is my brother we're talking about. Ramón Dario—soon to be second in the media mogul stakes only to my *papá*.'

That was exactly what Estrella had expected, if she was honest. But it was not what Ramón had wanted, it seemed. In fact so much of what Ramón wanted was the exact opposite of what she had anticipated that she was beginning to wonder whether the man she had agreed to marry was even the same one she'd met on that first day when he'd come to the castle to negotiate the purchase of the television company.

For a start there had been the engagement ring.

Knowing that their marriage was just to be a business arrangement, with nothing of any real feeling in it, apart from the blazing passion that Ramón had so openly admitted had driven him to propose, she had expected that they would go through the motions, nothing more. Her father would expect her to wear a ring; Ramón would provide one. That was all.

It was not all.

Not only had Ramón organised a very special ring for her he had organised an equally special event at which to give it to her. A party to which he had invited all his family, his friends, and everyone from Estrella's own family too.

'But why?' she asked him one evening in his apartment when he raised the idea of the party, and asked whom she wanted to invite. 'Why go to all this trouble for what is, after all, just an arranged marriage?'

Ramón looked at her, strangely cold, unemotional silvery eyes narrowed in sharp assessment.

'No one arranged this for me,' he returned, his tone sharp-edged. 'I proposed to you of my own choice—it was my decision and mine alone.'

'But—but…'

Estrella didn't know what to say. There were words inside her head, but they weren't words she felt safe or happy sharing.

No one had arranged their marriage—but they might have done. There was no emotion in their union, no form of feeling. Only lust and a need for a name—and, of course, the financial deal that Ramón wanted from her father. It was not a love match—and as such not a proper marriage. The bitterness that slashed at her soul with that thought made her bite her tongue sharply, preferring to suffer the small, self-inflicted pain, rather than let the truth come out.

'But what?' Ramón questioned savagely.

'Do—do you want to go to all this trouble for something that isn't a real marriage?'

'But it is a real marriage—as real a marriage as I'm ever going to have. Tell me something,' he snapped suddenly. 'Are you ashamed of this engagement?'

'Ashamed?' Estrella echoed, astounded that he should even think so. 'No—not at all, why should I be?'

'Well, we've already acknowledged the fact that I was not exactly number one on your list of would-be suitors...'

So that still rankled. Somehow Estrella suppressed the faint, ambiguous smile that tugged at the corners of her mouth. Ramón Dario was a proud, proud man. He hated the fact that he had come tenth on that infamous list.

'On my father's list,' she put in, but Ramón ignored her interjection.

'And I'm not a pure-bred Catalan—not pure-bred anything, if it comes to that.'

'Esteban Ramirez is pure-bred Catalan,' Estrella reminded him. 'And I dread to think how my life would have been if I'd ended up with him. My father may obsess about blood lines and ancestry, but I certainly don't. I wouldn't have ended up with—'

Suddenly horrified by the way that her tongue had almost run away with her, she slapped a hand across her mouth to silence herself, big dark eyes widening in shock above her concealing fingers.

'With Carlos,' Ramón finished for her. His use of the other man's name was flat and unrevealing, giving nothing away.

But suddenly Estrella's conscience stabbed at her savagely, telling her that she couldn't keep quiet any longer. That she had to tell him. She could face her father with defiance, tough it out in front of the gossips, pretend she didn't hear the whispers behind her back.

But not with Ramón.

There was something about this man that demanded openness and the truth—nothing less. She couldn't lie to him, couldn't conceal her feelings as she had learned to do with everyone else. When she was with him, it was as if he had ripped off the carefully concealing mask that she had struggled to fasten over her own features, scraping away the thin veneer of calm control and exposing the raw and vulnerable woman, the real Estrella, beneath.

'I didn't know Carlos was married,' she said suddenly, blurting out the words before she had a chance for any second thoughts that might destroy the tattered remnants of courage she had gathered round her.

The look Ramón turned on her was speculative rather than sceptical, but it still caught on her nerves that seemed to be missing a much-needed, protective layer of skin, leaving her raw and intensely vulnerable to what she saw as his disapproval.

'I didn't!' she reiterated. 'He told me he wasn't!'

'And you believed him?'

'Yes.'

It was just a whisper, but perhaps not for the reason he might think. The real shock that resounded in her mind, in her heart, was the realisation that something had changed.

The betrayal, the pain that Carlos had inflicted on her was still there. But somehow now she was seeing it differently. In a weird way, in her mind, it was as if she were viewing the past through the wrong end of a telescope, so that instead of seeming so much nearer, it looked as if it had gone further away. And because of the distance, her hurt was so much less.

It had been happening ever since Ramón had come into her life. At first, he had distracted her, giving her something else to think about. Then he had driven her to distraction with the way that she couldn't get him out of her mind. She had hoped that by going to his home that night she might have driven the troubling thoughts of him away, but in fact the opposite had happened. Ramón filled her mind so much that nothing else could make an impact on her feelings. He was an obsession—the first thought that slid into her mind on waking; the last thing to leave it at night.

'Yes, I believed him.'

And now she expected him to believe her too, Ramón told himself, wishing he didn't have to. She couldn't see that he'd been prepared to forget about the past, that what mattered was what they had between them. Instead, she'd made up this ridiculous story—this lie. Because it had to be a lie.

Of course she had known that Perea had been married. How could she not have done? Everyone had known. Even here, in Barcelona, the story had seeped out, the scandal and the way that Alfredo's fierce Catalan pride had been dragged in the dust by his wayward daughter.

The wayward daughter who was now going to be his wayward wife.

The wife who couldn't even honour him with the truth, but slanted the story so that she appeared in the best possible light. She was still lying, still using him...

But right now he didn't care. He wanted this woman in his bed, and if marrying her was the only way he was going to get her there, then marriage it would be.

'Oh, hell.'

Ramón reached out and roughly pulled her towards him, enclosing her in a bear hug that drove all the breath from her lungs. While she was still struggling to breathe normally, he put a hand under her chin and forced her face up to his, his proud head coming down, his hard mouth taking hers in a crushing, driven kiss.

'I'll make you forget him!' he muttered harshly against her lips. 'I'll wipe his image from your mind, all thought of him from your soul. You'll never think of him again—never—ever!'

'I...' Estrella tried, but any attempt to speak was cut off, crushed back down her throat by the force of another of those powerful, almost cruel kisses.

'You're mine, Doña Estrella—mine and no one else's. For as long as my ring is on your finger, you have my name, share my home, then you are mine and mine alone. Mine.'

He punctuated the word with another brutally demanding kiss that made her feel as if she were some slave of old, branded with her owner's mark, made permanently, ineradicably his.

'Mine—mine!'

It was all she wanted, Estrella acknowledged, deep inside. The dark, primitively carnal response that boiled up inside her at his touch was all that she could handle—all she needed right now. It had a savage force that took possession of her, drove all other thoughts from her mind, left her incapable of anything. It reduced her to a trembling, shaking wreck, to someone without a thought in her head, except for one.

And that was that she wanted this man.

Dear Lord, how she wanted him.

He only had to appear in sight and her blood heated in her veins. Only had to look at her and she was lost—to touch her and she went up in flames. She lived her life in a state of permanent meltdown.

It should have been scary. A year—a couple of months ago—she would have sworn that it would have terrified her. But now it didn't.

It was wonderful. It was exciting, exhilarating. It was like flying high up in a cloudless sky, with the warm sun on her face. It was being alive. She hadn't felt that way in a long, long time, even before she had met Carlos. And being with Carlos had never made her feel this way.

'I'm yours,' she told him, her mouth softening under his, returning the kiss, with interest.

Within seconds, as always happened, the kiss turned to need, the need to passion. The meal they had been planning was discarded, forgotten in the flaring heat of a very different sort of hunger, and they stumbled up the stairs, still kissing, snatching at each other's clothes until they tumbled onto the bed, mindless and heedless in the control of the insatiable hunger that simply being with each other could spark off between them.

Estrella's skin still flamed at just the memory now as she looked down at the ring that Ramón had placed on her hand at the party a couple of nights later. Softly she touched it, smoothing her fingertips over the beautiful, brilliant diamonds set in the shape of a star, a deliberate play on the meaning of her name. She had never expected anything like it. Never dreamed that he would come up with something so spectacular and stunning.

'I—I don't know how to thank you...' she stammered when the congratulations died down, the handshakes and the slaps on the back that Ramón received eased and they were at last able to snatch a few moments on their own in a quiet corner of the huge room in his father's house.

But Ramón dismissed her thanks with an arrogant wave of one strong hand, his eyes hooded, his expression strangely distant and unreadable.

'You're my fiancée. Naturally I would give you a ring. After all, we don't want anyone thinking that this engagement isn't real. Certainly not your father.'

But the mention of her father made Estrella flinch inside. She didn't want to think of the reason why Don Medrano had suddenly taken to smiling. Why he had even turned a couple of positively benign looks on his disappointing daughter—and even more approving ones on his soon-to-be son-in-law.

'My father's just grateful that he's getting rid of his shameful daughter. And he thinks you're wonderful because you're taking me off his hands in spite of my reputation as a scarlet woman.'

The sudden frown that drew Ramón's black brows sharply together was like a stab from the point of a painfully sharp knife. She knew that her voice had sounded petulant, even aggressive, but she hadn't been able to stop herself. She knew all about the hours that Ramón had spent closeted in the library with Alfredo and his lawyer, the secret negotiations that had gone on there to decide her fate. Ramón had given her no details, but her father had. She knew all about the bargain that Alfredo had offered as his share of the deal that they had all made between them. So she was sure that Ramón had emerged from the room as the new owner of the television company that he had wanted so much—at half the price he had planned to buy it in the first place.

'Perhaps I'm taking you because you are a scarlet woman,' Ramón drawled mockingly, his eyes gleaming silver as they slid down over the slender shape of her body in the clinging black and gold dress she wore tonight. 'Certainly, the scarlet woman is the one I like having in my life—the one I most enjoy taking to bed.'

The smile that lingered at the corners of his mouth as the words died away told her that he was thinking of the times she had visited his apartment, the heated way those evenings had been spent—and more often than not the mornings and the afternoons too.

'No matter how many times we come together, I still can never get enough of you.'

To prove his point he drew her towards him, his arms coming tight around her, pressing her close against the hard, strong length of his body. So close that she couldn't be unaware of the swollen, burning evidence of just how fiercely, potently aroused he was even now.

Instantly her own body responded, the biting hunger that was always with her whenever he touched, whenever she even thought of him, uncoiling in the pit of her stomach and sending shock waves of need radiating out along the line of each nerve, each cell. Every inch of her throbbed into heated demand, making her want to forget all her concerns, push them aside, hide them under the rush of sensuality that he could awaken so easily in her. But still with that secret business meeting in the forefront of her mind, Estrella found that, no matter how much she might want to, she still couldn't bite back the bitter response that rose to her lips.

'That's just as well—because I don't want you thinking that you can renege on our bargain.'

'And why would I want to do that, my beautiful star?'

Leaning forward, Ramón pressed his lips to her forehead, along the fine dark line of her brows, on the delicate vein that pulsed at her temple.

'Well, now you have what you want, you could—'

'You think I would go back on my promise—that I would break my word to you?'

His tone sharpened dangerously, his eyes flashing angry fire as they burned down into her wide, darkly shadowed ones.

'Don't you know that I would rather die than do that?'
Rather die…

The words made her head spin, her foolish, naïve heart

leaping at the sound of them; at the thought that she might actually mean more to him than just the wife acquired as a necessary part of a business deal. But even as the wild fantasy formed in her head Ramón's next words dashed it away again with a dousing of cold reason, as effective as the splash of icy water right in her face.

'If I give my word, it is a point of honour never to go back on it,' he declared tersely, each word snapped off in a harsh slash of sound. 'And besides, your father is no fool. His signature will not go on that vital piece of paper until mine is on our wedding certificate. So you need have no fear that I will run out on you before our wedding day, *querida*. I know too well what I want in life to do that.'

'Because you see the whole thing as a business arrangement.'

That brought her another swift, reproving glare from those steel-grey eyes, all the mockery leaching from them, leaving them cold and bleak as ice.

'I don't sleep with my business partners, Doña Medrano. I never have, and I don't intend to start now.'

'Then why—?'

But their private time was up. Mercedes spotted them in their corner and the next moment she and Cassie came over, Ramón's sister-in-law pulling him onto the dance floor, and the chance to talk was gone.

They didn't get it back either. There was more dancing, a meal, toasts and speeches followed and Estrella seemed to spend all her time forcing herself to thank well-wishers, accepting their congratulations with as much enthusiasm as she could manage, praying that her smile looked genuine and not as forced and as stiff as it felt to her.

By the end of the evening her jaw and cheek muscles ached and she had a pounding headache from trying to play the part of the happy, excited bride-to-be when inside she was feeling so tangled and messed up that she felt she would never be able to think straight again. She had danced with Ramón, spending long minutes in his arms, pressed hard against the taut muscles of his lean frame. And those minutes had stirred all her senses, making her long for the end of the evening when the prospect of being alone with him offered so much more than just a chance to talk.

But Ramón was suddenly a very different man. To the guests at the party he might seem exactly the same, smiling easily, talking even more so. He laughed, he told jokes, he played the role of the proud, happy fiancé to perfection. But to someone as sensitive to his every mood, to every nuance of his voice, his look, as Estrella had become, it was so obvious that he wasn't really there.

His eyes were strangely opaque, reflecting none of the warmth that was threaded through his voice, that curled his mouth in a wide, brilliant smile. When he touched her it was like being held by a stranger. Worse, it was like being in the arms of some brilliantly designed, almost human, but totally unfeeling animatronic creation that functioned in every way that a real person should but was somehow totally lacking in soul.

He held her, danced with her, but he didn't really touch her. He made polite, trivial conversation, listened to her responses, answered them, but didn't truly seem to hear her. Although he rarely left her side through what was left of the night, she never, ever felt that she had the real Ramón there, rather than some pale shadow of the man who was her fiancé, her lover, her prospective husband and yet whom she didn't truly know in any way at all.

The longed-for private time didn't come either. They had hardly said goodbye to the last, lingering guests when a gesture from Ramón's hand brought a maid hurrying up with Estrella's coat. Another summoned the chauffeur, who had obviously been waiting for just this command, and had a large, luxurious car purring at the main door in the blink of an eyelid, it seemed.

'But I...' Estrella tried to protest, but Ramón paid no heed to her stumbling attempt to dissuade him.

'I promised your father I would make sure you got home safely,' was all he would say. 'And as I have drunk too much champagne to drive you myself, then Paco will take care of you.'

'I thought—I'm not ready to leave yet!'

'Estrella...' Ramón's voice sounded appallingly reasonable, even gentle, though his cold eyes and the hard set of his jaw delivered exactly the opposite message. 'It's been a long night, and we have a busy week coming up, preparing for the wedding.'

Softly he touched her face, trailing his fingers down the line of her cheek, and it was only looking into those hooded eyes that kept her from turning her head and pressing her lips into the centre of his hard palm.

'I'm not tired.'

'And I want to make sure you stay that way. I want a glowing bride on our wedding day, not someone pale and worn out from lack of sleep.'

'But...'

'Estrella—you are going home.'

He didn't raise his voice, it remained cold and flat, but somehow so brutally emphatic that she knew she didn't dare to argue. She certainly didn't want to risk saying that she had hoped to stay with him tonight. That she needed his arms around her, his kiss on her lips.

'Oh, all right. If you insist.'

The kiss, she tried for, standing on tiptoe and pressing her mouth against the lean, stubble-shadowed plane of his cheek, his lips. But there was no response. If it hadn't been for the warmth of his skin, the yielding softness of his flesh, she would have thought that he was surrounded by a sheet of plate glass, cold and hard and totally unwelcoming. He didn't even kiss her back, but reached for the long, black velvet evening coat the maid held and wrapped it round Estrella's shoulders, pulling it close at her neck.

'Goodnight, *querida*. Sleep well.'

Taking her arm, he almost hustled her down the steps and into the waiting car, barely giving her time to settle on the soft leather of the wide back seat before he slammed shut the door and straightened up again.

Still she tried to wave—to blow him a kiss—but he just rapped on the driver's window to order him to start, then stepped back, his stunning face carefully blanked off as he watched the car pull away. A second later he had turned on his heel, marched up the steps, and was gone.

Although she had seen him on several occasions since, he had never once taken her to bed again since that night. He had always been perfectly polite, sociable even, but he had made sure that they were rarely on their own together, and if they were it was in some place where they couldn't do more than kiss, and certainly not make love.

So tonight—their wedding night—was something that Estrella was looking forward to with a strong sense of apprehension, almost as much as if she had been a virgin anticipating her husband's lovemaking for the very first time.

Looking down at the beautiful diamond star engagement ring that shone on her finger, she touched it softly, her eyes blurring faintly, her expression thoughtful.

Which Ramón would she be with tonight? The ardent, passionate lover who couldn't keep his hands off her, or the strangely subdued, distant and withdrawn man he had become since the night of their engagement party? She didn't know, and not knowing was twisting her nerves into tight, painful knots, making her heart lurch into an uncomfortable, urgent beat, pounding unevenly in double-quick time.

Restlessly she twisted the ring round and round on her finger, betraying the unease and discomfort of her thoughts.

'Estrella!'

It was Mercedes' voice, dragging her back from the uncomfortable place that her reflections had taken her to, making her head come up with a start, her dark eyes widen in stunned shock.

'I—I'm sorry,' she managed awkwardly, struggling for control again. 'I was miles away.'

'And I know where!' Mercedes grinned. 'You've really got it bad! I wonder if that brother of mine knows just how madly in love with him you are.'

'Wha...?'

Estrella's head jerked in shock and she tried to speak, but the word died in the middle, her throat drying, her tongue seizing up as the impact of what Mercedes had said really hit home.

Love.

Had Mercedes said love?

Her mind reeled as if the words had been a violent blow struck right in her face, and she couldn't gather her scattered thoughts together to focus on the word and the problems it brought with it.

Problems that would change the whole of the rest of her life.

She could only be thankful that Mercedes had chosen that moment to turn away, looking for her handbag, and so never saw the way that all colour leached from Estrella's face, leaving her eyes looking like two huge, dark bruises above her pale, wan cheeks.

I wonder if that brother of mine knows just how madly in love with him you are.

Oh, heaven help her, what did she do now?

CHAPTER TEN

'SHE'LL be here soon.'

Joaquin grinned widely at his brother as they stood to one side of the altar in the small village church.

'You'd better enjoy your last moments of freedom.'

'Says the man who's only been married a month or so himself,' laughed Alex, the youngest of Juan Alcolar's three sons. 'As an old married man, myself, I can heartily recommend it.'

He meant it too, Ramón reflected, seeing the way that Alex's dark grey eyes sought out the tall, slender, brown-haired figure of his English wife Louise, who sat just a few metres away in one of the family pews, her baby daughter on her lap. Ever since Alex had returned from a visit to England with Louise and some story of her claiming to be his wife, the two of them had been inseparable. Now the birth of Maria Elena had put the crown on their love.

Joaquin too had found happiness, though it had been a close-run thing. before his older half-brother had finally seen sense and realised that he was madly in love with Cassie. Now they were married, with their first child on the way. Joaquin had mellowed too, his once prickly relationship with both his father and Ramón himself becoming easier, more relaxed, as he settled into his new way of life. Knowing he loved and was loved had turned him from the man some had called *El Lobo*—the Lone Wolf—into a very different personality.

Privately Ramón admitted to being jealous as hell. His brothers were both living out the happy ever after that he had once believed was an impossibility. The happy ever after that, if he was honest, he had once wanted for himself.

His own home life, growing up with his mother dead and the man he believed was his father a harsh, aggressive, unloving figure, had made him long for the sort of family his friends had had. He'd vowed that one day, when he was a man, he would find that life, create the sort of home he had never known, with a wife he loved and centred his life around.

So why was he marrying Estrella? Why was he standing here, today, with his brothers, wearing the traditional tucked and hand-finished shirt that, to his total astonishment, Estrella had insisted on making for him?

'I have to admit I'm stunned,' Alex was saying now. 'If anyone got you down the aisle, I always thought it would be the lovely Benita. One minute you only had eyes for her. The next, you announced that you were marrying some woman we'd never heard of. What the devil happened?'

'Estrella happened,' Ramón returned, knowing he spoke nothing less than the truth.

He'd asked himself that same question heaven knew how many times, and never come up with any other more coherent answer.

Estrella had happened. She had burst into his life like a blazing comet rather than the star that gave her her name, and he hadn't been able to think straight ever since. Benita, who had seemed the most desirable female he knew up until that moment, now never crossed his mind. He couldn't even bring her features to mind if he tried—not that he ever did try. His thoughts were fully occupied with images of the woman he was going to marry today.

'Mercedes always said that if you ever fell in love, you'd fall hard,' Joaquin put in. 'But she was sure that you were going to be a long time finding someone you wanted to be with.'

'Mercedes thinks she knows too much,' Ramón scoffed, hoping that he sounded convincing.

He'd fallen hard, all right—but not in love. He was head over heels in lust and he couldn't break free from the sensual chains that Estrella had fastened around him. He wasn't at all sure he wanted to either.

But that wasn't being in love. It was something else entirely.

He was no longer sure he believed in love, not for himself. Oh, he had done once, when he was younger. It was only later, when he had discovered that he was not his father's child, that his mother had been unfaithful early on in her marriage, and he had been the result, that disillusionment had set in.

'Our little sister needs to know what love is all about before she starts propounding on how it will affect other people's lives.'

'Well, that might not be too long coming,' was his elder brother's response. 'She's been hopelessly distracted these past few days. Maybe she has someone on her mind.'

'Well, if she does, heaven help us,' Alex put in devoutly. 'Mercedes feels passionately enough about the most ordinary things. Remember how she once thought she was in love with me when I first turned up—before she realised I was actually her brother? If she ever fell in love for real then she would be in deep right from the start.'

'That seems to be something of a family trait,' Joaquin murmured dryly. 'It's just that some of us take a while to discover the truth.'

And some of us settle for other things instead, Ramón reflected, though he didn't actually voice the words. He didn't feel that his brothers, so sure of their own feelings and those of their wives, would understand the way he was acting—the reasons that had brought him here today.

But one thing was true. He had been in deep from the start—and he was getting in deeper with every day that passed. And that was why he was here. Not for any damn business deal, or because Estrella had asked him, or because of the aristocratic inheritance that might be in the future for any children he might have.

He was here because he couldn't stay away. Because of all the things he had wanted out of this arrangement, all that he would acquire as a result of it, Estrella was what he wanted most of all.

'She's here.'

He wasn't sure which brother actually said the words, only knew that the subdued flurry of excitement and interest at the far end of the church meant that Estrella, his bride—soon to be his wife—had arrived. The time for second thoughts, if he was to have any, was now.

Surprisingly, perhaps, there were none. Nothing at all but a calm, deep conviction that this was what he wanted. This was what was right for him. For now—and he'd let the future take care of itself.

'Here we go.'

It was Joaquin this time. His elder half-brother checked Ramón's appearance, tweaked his cravat into place, slapped him on the shoulder.

'Showtime, *hermano*.'

And it was that *hermano*—that 'brother'—that rocked him. After all the tensions there had been in their relationship until now, tensions that were inevitable in the unconventional set-up of their family, the unexpected term of affection, and the grin that accompanied it, left him with his mind reeling for a moment. Relief, delight, gratitude flooded his thoughts so that at first he missed the beginnings of a minor sensation at the bride's appearance.

'Oh, Lord…'

Alex's muttered comment under his breath was what penetrated his hearing first. That and the note of stunned disbelief, blending with a wicked, amused delight, brought him back to reality in a rush.

'Ramón?'

What?

The murmurs and the whispers behind him grew, the sound swelling, rising towards him as if on a wave, getting louder, becoming impossible to ignore.

Ramón couldn't stand at the altar with his back to the rest of the church any longer. He had to turn, had to look.

Oh, dear God, but she was beautiful!

That was his first thought; the only thought that registered for a moment. Just the sight of her took his breath away, making his head spin dangerously.

She was so, so beautiful. As soon as he saw her his body responded, hard and fast, in a definitely carnal, definitely non-spiritual way. A way that was totally inappropriate to his place here, at the foot of the altar steps.

She was alone, having refused the idea of her father giving her away. She wasn't wearing any veil or headdress, but she had piled her gleaming jet hair up on the top of her head, and it was scattered all over with tiny white flowers. Her face was slightly pale, but resolute, and her deep ebony eyes looked huge and darker than ever in contrast. As soon as he turned those wide eyes fastened on his face, watching him intently, a little hint of more colour creeping into her porcelain cheeks.

The way she had pulled her hair up exposed the long, elegant line of her neck, broken only by the finest of gold chains with a star-shaped diamond pendant hanging from it.

A diamond pendant that exactly matched her engagement ring and that he had sent to her only the night before, as his wedding gift to his bride. It sat perfectly at the base of her throat, revealed by the square-cut neckline of her dress. The square-cut neckline that had been the only thing she had told him about what she was going to wear.

The square-cut neckline of the long, fitted, silken...

His eyes dropped lower, taking in what she was wearing, and then swung back up to her face, his dark head going back in shock.

'Oh, Estrella!' Ramón breathed, her name breaking on a note of stunned laughter, of pride, of amazement. 'Oh, *mi Estrella!*'

My father's just grateful that he's getting rid of his shameful daughter. Estrella's words, spoken on the night of their engagement party, sounded loud and clear inside his head. *And he thinks you're wonderful because you're taking me off his hands in spite of my reputation as a scarlet woman.*

He knew that there had been talk. That interfering gossips from the village, her father, an elderly, scandalised aunt, had made comments about what she might wear to her wedding. That they had said that the traditional white might not be appropriate. They had suggested cream, or perhaps blue...

And Estrella had listened, and kept her own counsel, and never given a clue as to what she'd been planning. So that now she had hit them right between the eyes.

The dress was long, sweeping down to the floor as most traditional wedding dresses did. It was made of the finest, most supple silk available, and it was as beautifully cut, as supremely elegant, as he would have expected from anything that Estrella chose. The tight-fitting bodice, with the square neckline she had described, contrasted with the swathe of silk, the long train that fell from her slender waist.

It was the perfect traditional wedding dress in design—in all but one thing.

No traditional wedding dress had ever been made in such a bold, brilliant colour. No traditional dress would ever have been in such a stunning, undeniable, hit-you-right-between-the-eyes scarlet.

My scarlet woman.

My bold, my brilliant, my brave Estrella.

Ramón didn't know if he actually spoke the words or if they only sounded inside his head. He just knew that he couldn't stand here, waiting, seeing the way she had hesitated, the sudden uncertainty in her eyes.

Before he was even aware that he was moving, he had left his place at the altar and was striding down the aisle towards her, his hand coming out, reaching for hers.

Immediately all the uncertainty, the apprehension fled from her face. Her smile was wide, stunning, dazzling, and she took her bouquet in one hand, holding the other out to him, that amazing smile growing as he folded his fingers around it.

'My scarlet woman! My beautiful scarlet woman.'

This time he did say the words, but in a whisper that only the two of them could hear, and he lifted her hand to his lips, pressing a warm, ardent kiss on the backs of her fingers before moving to her side, tucking the hand he had kissed under his arm and smiling down at her in his turn. He saw the faint glisten of tears in the huge dark eyes she turned on him and knew that, for all the bravado that had stiffened her back, lifted her head high, made her walk tall and proud down that aisle, the focus of all eyes, she had not been as confident as she had looked. She had been brave and determined, but quailing just a little inside.

So he squeezed her hand, pressing his own bigger, broader one on top of the slender, delicate fingers that lay

on his arm, pale against the darkness of the cloth of his
morning coat. And he smiled at her again, seeing her confidence grow in response as she swallowed down the betraying moisture.

'Ready?' he murmured and she nodded. Firm, sure, positively resolved this time, there was no hesitation, not a
flicker of doubt in her face.

'Ready,' she echoed, and moved forward with him, perfectly in step towards the waiting priest.

Estrella felt as if she were floating on air. Her feet barely
seemed to touch the ground as she walked the last steps to
the altar, Ramón's tall, powerful form at her side, the
strength of his arm supporting her, his hand on hers.

She had arrived at the church in a state that had been
almost sick with nerves. Mercedes' words had hit home like
a bolt of lightning, illuminating everything she hadn't seen
or understood before.

*You've really got it bad! I wonder if that brother of mine
knows just how madly in love with him you are.*

Once she had let the words into her thoughts, she couldn't
drive them away again. No matter how hard she tried to
distract herself, to think of other things, she still kept coming
back to that one forceful word. The one that had the power
to rock her world and turn everything she had believed upside down.

Love.

She had tried to deny it. Had tried to find arguments to
refute it, reasons why it was wrong, wrong, wrong. But it
wasn't.

Instead it was right, right, right. Though she had no idea
how it had happened.

But in the moment that she had begun the long, nerve-
shattering walk down the aisle she had known that it was
nothing less than the truth. Each step that she took neare

and nearer to where Ramón stood, strong, straight-backed, dark head held proudly high, broad shoulders set square under the perfect tailoring of his morning coat, also took her closer and closer to the need to face her destiny.

She had fallen blindly, crazily, headlong and irrevocably in love with Ramón Dario, the bridegroom her father had bought for her.

It was nothing like what she had felt for Carlos. In fact it was so unlike those feelings that she knew she had to admit to the truth. What she had felt for Carlos had in fact not been love at all. It had been nothing more than a blind infatuation, a loss of all sense, a falling in love with the idea of being in love. She had thought she had cared for him, but, compared with the huge, swamping tidal wave that was her feelings for Ramón, her passion for Carlos had been nothing more than a brief, ineffectual cloudburst, over and gone again in the space of a few brief moments.

What she felt for Ramón was so different. It was rooted deep in her heart, part of her lifeblood, her soul. She couldn't root it out and still live. Without him she would be nothing, and there would be no future for her.

At that realisation her footsteps had faltered, slowed. She hadn't known if she could go any further. Her legs had felt unsteady beneath her, her knees had shaken. A cold shudder of panic had run down her spine and if she had had the strength she would have turned tail and run—right out of the church.

But in that moment Ramón had turned and looked at her.

He had done more. He had walked towards her, his hand held out. He had taken her fingers in his, hard and strong, and infinitely comforting and warm.

'My scarlet woman!' he had said. 'My beautiful scarlet woman.'

It wasn't much, perhaps. It certainly wasn't everything

she was dreaming of. It was no powerful, ardent declaration of love. But then she had never expected that. And when she compared those words, spoken in a deep, husky voice, with the ring of total commitment behind them, with the flowery, over-the-top, insincere flattery that Carlos had used on her, she knew which she infinitely preferred. Which she believed in most.

When he had smiled at her, she had felt she would go anywhere with him. If she had doubted before, now she knew she really loved him, rather than just being in love with him.

And Ramón?

She knew why he was marrying her. They were starting out on their life together for all the wrong reasons—financial, not emotional. It was a marriage of convenience, but that didn't mean it had to stay that way. It was also a marriage of passion—intense, physical passion, and as long as they had that, they had something that would hold them together.

And if she couldn't work on that, then she was an idiot.

'As long as this lasts, we'll stay together,' Ramón had said. 'Until we all get what we want.'

Well, he already had what he wanted financially—or he would have by the end of today. But he wanted her as well, he had made that so blazingly clear. His hunger for her was the ace she held in her hand. As long as he wanted her, they would stay together.

And as long as they stayed together, there was always a chance that he would come to feel more for her than just the ardent passion he openly acknowledged. She'd make sure she kept that passion alive. She'd feed it, watch it grow, pray it chained him to her in fetters of burning need.

It was enough to start with; she could only pray that

given time, and the kindness of fate, it would turn into something much more.

That was the thought that kept her going throughout the long ceremony, the reception afterwards. She could do nothing now, but tonight, when they were alone together in the villa overlooking the sea on the Costa Brava that Juan Alcolar had loaned them for the first night of their honeymoon, she would start to forge those chains in the heat and hunger of their marriage bed.

It could work; she knew it could.

It would work! It had to.

Because if it didn't, then this marriage was going nowhere. If she couldn't change the desire that Ramón felt for her into something deeper, stronger, then one day, inevitably, without love to sustain it, that desire would fade and there would be nothing left. Then she would lose him. He would turn and walk away from her for ever.

But before then, she had time. And she was going to use that time in the best way that she could.

Starting with tonight.

CHAPTER ELEVEN

THANK God that things were almost over, Ramón told himself in fervent relief.

If he had to spend another hour—another moment—making polite conversation, accepting congratulations, smiling acknowledgement of jokes in dubious taste about loss of freedom, the prospect of the wedding night to come, then he would explode.

It wasn't that he hadn't enjoyed the reception—he had—at the start. He'd enjoyed being with his family, dancing with Estrella, with Cassie, with Mercedes, and ultimately with Estrella again. But enough was enough. He had had more than enough of socialising, being on show.

He wanted to be alone—with his wife—in private.

His wife.

Looking across the huge ballroom, he saw where Estrella, resplendent in that stunning scarlet gown, was standing, laughing at something Mercedes had said to her. With her head thrown back, her dark eyes, and a wash of colour tinting her cheeks, she looked nothing like the pale, apprehensive slip of a creature who had appeared in the church earlier today. The brave, resolute Estrella who had been determined to show defiance, but who had been unable to hide her uncertainty at the last minute.

'She looks wonderful, doesn't she?'

His father had appeared at his side, wineglass in his hand. His deep brown eyes were fixed on Estrella too, but there was something in them that caught Ramón's attention, made him look more closely.

Juan Alcolar's voice had been faintly husky and his eyes had an unusual gleam in them that in another man might have looked suspiciously like the glisten of tears.

Or they would have been if his father was the sort of man who betrayed his emotions, Ramón told himself. In fact the truth about Juan was the exact opposite. He rarely, if ever, let anyone in, not even his family. Not his sons, anyway; Mercedes could always charm him into a very different mood. It had been that way ever since they had first met, on that day, so many years before, when Ramón had marched into Juan Alcolar's office and demanded to know if what he had learned was the truth, if in fact Juan was his father and not the recently deceased Reuben Dario, the man whose son he had always believed he was.

'She reminds me of Honoria.'

Ramón turned his head sharply in shock, unable to believe what he was hearing. Honoria had been Juan's legal wife; the mother of Joaquin and Mercedes. He was surprised to find that his father would talk of her now, when he had never done so before.

'Did she look like Estrella?' he managed carefully.

'A lot.'

Juan drank deeply from the wine in his glass as if nerving himself to go on.

'Don't make the mistakes that I did, Ramón.'

'Mistakes?'

Ramón knew his voice had sharpened, wondered if it would drive his father back into his normal reticent silence, but still Juan seemed prepared to open up a little.

'I loved two women very dearly,' he said. 'And lost them both.'

'My mother…'

His father nodded sombrely.

'I adored Marguerite, but I was young—stupid. I said I

didn't want commitment or marriage and I broke her heart. That's why she married Reuben Dario.'

Why now? Ramón asked himself. Why, for perhaps only the second time in his life, had his father actually brought his mother into the conversation, even referring to her by name?

'But you saw her again.'

His own tone was rough, raw-edged.

'Just the once. We met by chance years later—I was married too by then, to Honoria, and Joaquin was almost two...'

His sigh was deep, dragged up from the depths of his heart.

'Nothing had changed. She was still the most beautiful woman I had ever seen—the woman of my dreams. And she was lost, lonely. She and Dario had never been able to have children and her marriage was on the rocks. I'm not proud of what happened. We spent one week together while Reuben was away in America. One wonderful week. But we both knew it couldn't last. Neither of us could live with the guilt—the thought of what we were doing to others. So we parted.'

The last of the wine in his glass was emptied, the muscles in his throat working hard to swallow.

'You were born nine months later.'

'And my mother had died before I was two months old.'

He had no memory of her. Only the image of her face in photographs he had seen.

'But you soon forgot her,' he said, unable to keep the bitterness out of his voice. 'Soon had someone else. Alex is only a year younger than me.'

'No!' his father put in, rough and raw. 'It wasn't like that. I went completely off the rails—I didn't know—didn't care what I was doing. On a business trip to England, there was a woman—the housekeeper in a place I visited. She looked just like your mother—like Marguerite when we first met. I got very drunk—it was a one-night stand. I didn't even know she was ever pregnant. Not until Alex turned up.'

'Then who?'

Estrella had finished her conversation and she was looking around the room, searching for someone. As he watched she caught sight of him, smiled in a way that made his head spin, and headed in his direction.

'Who was the other woman I loved? Who do you think? Honoria—my wife—Joaquin and Mercedes' mother.'

'But I always understood that that was an arranged marriage.'

'It was—to start with. I didn't realise what I had.'

'Then it's Joaquin you should be talking to about this.'

'I did—on his wedding day. He was the one who asked me to tell you too.'

'He did?'

Estrella was coming closer. Another couple of moments and she would be with them. Just looking at her made it almost impossible to concentrate.

'You're so much like me, Ramón. Joaquin knows that too. We both want you to be happy.'

'I am…'

Suddenly he wished he had a glass of wine too. His throat seemed to have dried painfully, making it impossible to get the last word out.

'What mistakes?' he growled, his eyes on the beautiful, scarlet figure of his wife.

'I didn't give enough.' His father hadn't needed him to elaborate, explain what he meant. 'I had what I wanted, but I didn't give any of them the commitment they needed until it was too late.'

'Well, you've no need to worry…'

Hastily he let the muttered assurance die as Estrella came

to his side, sliding a hand into his arm just as she had in the church. Just the feel of her soft touch made his heart kick, and the scent of her perfume in his nostrils sent his senses rushing into overdrive.

'No need to worry about what?' she asked with quiet curiosity.

'To worry about us,' Ramón answered hastily, unsure whether Juan might say something awkward. 'My father thought we should be leaving so that we aren't making the drive to the villa in the middle of the night.'

Looking down into her upturned face, he touched one fingertip to her cheek, smoothed it over the lush shape of her mouth.

'And I think so too.' His voice deepened, became thick and husky. 'It's time we began our married life together.'

'I agree.'

Something in her voice, her smile, made desire clutch at him and he knew that unless they were alone together soon he would go completely crazy with need. It was a relief to hear Estrella add the words, 'I only have to change into something more suitable for travelling and I'm all yours.'

All yours! Oh, God, did she know what those words, the tone she used, did to him? He was willing to bet that she did and just knowing that brought his pulse rate up, tightening the knots of tension inside another notch.

If he hadn't known better, if she hadn't been in his sight all day, he would have sworn that something had happened to her. Something that had changed her subtly, but dramatically, made her into a very different person.

'Go and get changed then,' he managed huskily.

Then, because he couldn't resist it, he dropped a kiss onto that soft, inviting mouth, taking it hard and fast. Hard because of the force of the feelings welling up inside him, and

KATE WALKER   139

fast because he didn't believe he could stop at a kiss, if he
lingered.

Especially when she responded so instantly, so wonderfully, so fully, her mouth opening under his, the tip of her
tongue sliding out and tracing along the soft line of his inner
lip, making him want to groan out loud in uncontrolled hunger.

Somehow he reined himself in, managed to resist the
temptation, taking only the one, lingering kiss before he
lifted his head again and looked deep into the wide, smoky
jet pools of her eyes.

'But don't take long about it. I'll be waiting...'

It was both a warning and a promise and he knew that
she had taken it that way when those huge eyes widened
even further and her sharp white teeth suddenly dug into
the pink flesh of her lower lip.

Suddenly he couldn't bear to see her hurt or damaged in
any way, even when it was only this tiny, self-inflicted pain.

'Don't,' he murmured, and when she froze, staring at him,
he bent and kissed away the small indentations, soothing
them with his tongue.

'Don't...' he said again, against her lips, hearing her
swiftly indrawn breath, feeling it on his own mouth.

'No,' she said in sighing acquiescence.

The erotic sparks that flashed between them were electric,
crackling in the air, so that he was sure his father and anyone else nearby must see them. He had to get her out of
here, get himself out with her before they gave into the
blazing, carnal impulses that throbbed through his body.

Reluctantly, he tore his mouth from hers. It was either
that or...

No! He mustn't think.

'Go and get changed, Señora Dario,' he commanded.
'And be quick about it.'

The sparkle in her eyes, the curve of her soft mouth were almost his undoing, but at least she stepped back a pace or two from him, giving him space to breathe, before she swept him a low, courtly, but clearly mocking curtsey.

'Of course, señor. As my husband commands.'

Witch! She knew just what she was doing, knew what effect she was having on him. He was torn between the need for a long drink to ease his parched mouth and throat and the total impossibility of looking anywhere but at the lithe movement of her body, the sway of her neat buttocks under the scarlet silk as she walked away from him. Watching her won out, as she obviously realised it would, and the moments when she mounted the stairs, heading for the room where her going-away outfit was laid out, was pure torture, an exercise in the sort of self-control that he'd never known he possessed.

He couldn't drag his eyes away until she reached a turn in the wide, curving staircase and, following it, disappeared from view. As she did so Ramón closed his eyes, holding the image inside his mind, projecting it onto the screen of his eyelids, preserving just for a moment longer. All he could think of was the moment that he would get her on her own with him, when he could peel off whatever she had decided to wear to go on honeymoon, reveal that perfect bottom to his hungry eyes and hands…his lips…

Commitment—hell, yes he was committed to this woman. He was trapped, a prisoner, and there was no way that he could get free. His father need have nothing to worry about. Nothing at all.

'Señor Dario—Ramón.' A voice at his side spoke, breaking into the sensual reverie—a voice he recognised, frowning.

'Don Alfredo?'

Reluctantly he forced his eyes open, looking straight into the cold, hooded gaze of his brand-new father-in-law.

'We have some business to finish, I believe.'

'Now?'

With an effort he crushed back the exclamation of annoyance and impatience that almost escaped him. Of course now. He had insisted on it himself. They would finalise the deal on the day he married Estrella, and then he wanted to hear no more about it.

'Of course. Do you have the papers?'

'Right here.'

The older man touched the breast pocket of his morning suit.

'And there is a room just there…'

He indicated with a wave of his hand.

'Where we have been assured we can have complete privacy.'

'All right, then.'

Ramón pushed both his hands through his hair, struggling to adjust his thoughts, drag them back to business mode and away from the darkly sensual path they still wanted to follow.

'Let's get this over with.'

Estrella hummed to herself as she slipped out of the tight-fitting scarlet dress and placed it on a silk-covered, padded hanger. A song from *West Side Story* kept playing over and over inside her head, its words reflecting exactly the way she felt.

She did feel pretty. So, so pretty—and stunning—and entrancing. How could she feel anything else, when she had seen the way that Ramón had looked at her, seen the barely restrained passion that had darkened his eyes, felt it in his kiss?

She might not yet be able to carol that she was loved by someone pretty wonderful, but she felt a whole new rush of hope, of optimism, of certainty that everything really, truly, had a chance of turning out all right.

Hugging herself tightly round the waist, she danced around the huge, luxurious bedroom, unable to contain her delight any more. She had to give it physical expression, spinning round and round in a wild, exhilarated circle until she collapsed in dizzied exhaustion on the silken coverlet of the enormous bed.

She would make Ramón love her, she vowed. She could do it! She really could.

But not if she lay here for much longer, she realised, pushing herself upwards in a rush and studying her reflection in the mirror. Professionally applied before her departure for the church, her make-up had lasted wonderfully. Perhaps if she just darkened her eye shadow a little—glossed her lips...

The repairs took only moments, and slipping into the elegant cream trouser suit with a tiny, black self-embroidered camisole top underneath was soon done. High-heeled sandals on her feet—and...

No.

She stilled the hand that she had raised to her hair, deciding against her original plan of removing the pins that held the elaborate style in place, combing out the orange blossom flowers and letting her black locks hang loose. Far better to leave it the way it was. It would be cooler, less trouble, on the journey, and when they reached the villa, then she would ask Ramón to help her let down the style. She knew how he loved to tangle his fingers in her hair, sensed intuitively that he would love the slow, gradual unpinning, the way that the loosened locks would tumble about her face, her shoulders. He could comb his fingers through it, kissing her at intervals...

It would be their own personal, sensual sort of foreplay. Already her mouth was dry, her body taut and thrumming with excitement, just thinking of it.

She couldn't wait any longer. A quick spritz of her favourite perfume scented the spots behind her ears, the pulse at the base of her neck, her cleavage. Then, snatching up her neat patent leather envelope-shaped bag, she headed out of the door and back down the stairs to the ballroom again, still singing.

She had just reached the curve on the staircase, the small half-landing where she could see the crowded room, but no one there could see her, when the sound of a door opening on the right drew her attention. What she saw froze her into stillness, her heart suddenly leaping up high in her throat.

Ramón.

Ramón and her father were just coming out of a side room. Together.

And that could only mean one thing.

It was like the afternoon they had spent closeted in the library together just a few weeks before. When they had...

No—she didn't want to think about it. She wished she hadn't seen.

But she had seen. And all the wishing in the world couldn't take her back a couple of minutes, back to the room, making her pause to adjust her jacket once more, or add another coating of mascara to her lashes, winding back time so that she left the bedroom, headed for the stairs just a moment or two later, and so hadn't seen.

Hadn't seen Ramón stalking out ahead of her father, still pushing a long, white envelope into the inside pocket of his elegant jacket. Hadn't seen her father clicking closed the fine gold pen in his hand before returning it to the breast pocket of his.

The wedding was over. The vows had been made. She and Ramón were man and wife—and so the legal details of the business deal had to be dealt with, the documents signed, contracts exchanged. He hadn't even bothered to wait until their wedding day was finished before he had insisted on the reward he had wanted for taking her on, saving her reputation. He might just as well have produced the financial contract in the church, to be signed in the first second after he had put his name to the marriage certificate.

There was a sensation like the stab of a dagger formed from pure ice right in the centre of her heart, so savage that she almost cried out in agony at it. But somehow, with a supreme effort, she managed to control it, biting down on her bottom lip so sharply that she felt the sudden, rusty taste of blood in her mouth.

'So you'll make him love you, will you, you little fool?' she whispered to herself, admitting that she'd let herself forget harsh reality while she'd been dreaming upstairs, building castles in the air. 'You're only deceiving yourself. You always knew what he wanted—and love doesn't come into it.'

Luckily, no one had seen her. She was hidden where she was and as long as she didn't move, no one would realise she was here.

So she stayed there, watching through a stinging veil of tears. Tears that she fought against hard, determined to hold them back, refusing to let them fall, no matter what the cost.

She would count to thirty and then she would go down, she told herself. Thirty seconds should be long enough.

'One…two…'

It was strange, she couldn't help reflecting, but, considering this had to be his moment of triumph, the time when he had won everything he'd wanted, everything he had married her for, Ramón didn't look the least bit exultant. Quite the opposite. A black frown, dark as a storm cloud seemed to have settled on his stunning features, drawing his strong, straight brows together, tightening the muscles in his mouth and jaw, until he looked as dangerous as a bomb primed to go off at any moment. It seemed that someone—her father, perhaps—had lit the blue touch-paper and stood well back, out of the range of the imminent explosion.

'Fourteen...'

Or was it twenty?

She had completely lost count. Didn't know what she was doing, or where she was. Perhaps she should start from the beginning again. Or—

'Estrella!'

There was no mistaking that voice or the ferocious impatience in it. Belatedly she realised that Ramón had moved to the foot of the stairs and was looking up at her. From here he could see her only too clearly—and he obviously wanted to know just what she was doing hovering at the top of the stairs, looking as if she had forgotten how to get down into the ballroom.

'Estrella!'

It was quieter this time, but no less forceful, the note he used making it plain that he was not prepared to hang around waiting for her while she dithered in indecision.

As she blinked away the blur that shock and confusion had filmed over her eyes she saw him move to the centre of the bottom step—no higher—and hold out his hand in a lordly, arrogant motion, summoning her to his side. He was not going to come up and fetch her, that gesture said. Her place was here, at his side, and she had better hurry up and join him.

Knowing only too well that hesitation would be interpreted as defiance, and that defiance was clearly something that would not be tolerated, Estrella hurried down the steps as quickly as the ridiculously high heels on her shoes would let her.

She had barely reached his side before his hand came out and clamped around hers, the powerful grip crushing the bones of her hand so that she winced in discomfort.

'Ready?' Ramón asked and his tone was so very, very different from the way that he had used it in the church—was it only five hours before?

'Y-yes.'

It was all she could manage. As he marched her across the room, almost dragging her in the wake of his long, angry strides, her thoughts were spinning, struggling to find some reason for this change of mind, not wanting to come up with the obvious.

But the obvious was all that sprang to mind.

Ramón had married her to acquire the television station he wanted. That and the aristocratic inheritance for any children perhaps. Now that he had what he wanted, then all pretence of caring for her in the least was off. It had to have been a pretence. Otherwise why would he look the way he did, with that cold fury turning his eyes molten, tightening his lips to just a thin, hard line?

Unless, of course, her father had pulled some underhand trick, perhaps going back on the deal he had promised.

But if he had, then what did that augur for the future of their marriage—if they had a marriage at all?

She didn't know, and Ramón was clearly in no mood to tell her. And now she was supposed to go away with this icily furious man. She was supposed to spend a honeymoon, more than two weeks alone, with this darkly dangerous stranger. Only a few minutes before she had viewed the prospect with delight and excited anticipation. Now all that excitement had fled from her like air from a punctured balloon, leaving her feeling limp and sick with dread.

Somehow she managed to make it to the door, though her legs were unsteady with apprehension beneath her. Somehow she managed to smile and hug and kiss and thank all the right people, though she could never have said exactly whom. Somehow she managed to get into the waiting limousine without stumbling or cracking her head on the roof.

Then, before she had time to settle either physically or emotionally, before she was in the slightest bit comfortable, Ramón slid onto the soft leather seat beside her, and rapped on the glass panel between them and the chauffeur.

'Okay,' was all he said.

And as Paco switched on the engine, put the car into gear, he slammed the door shut, shutting them together in the confined enclosed space.

CHAPTER TWELVE

'IS SOMETHING wrong?'

It was the second time that Estrella had asked the question, the first being as the sleek, powerful car had headed out of the city and onto the road heading north. Then Ramón hadn't been able to answer her. He still didn't want to. He was finding it difficult to speak, even to look at her.

'Don't talk, Estrella,' he said sharply. 'I don't feel like it.'

'Too much to drink?'

Her voice had a strangely jerky laugh in it, one that made the words come and go as if transmitted by a badly tuned radio.

'Too much something, that's for sure,' he muttered, leaning back in his seat and letting his head fall onto the rest, closing his eyes to shut out the world he no longer wanted to see.

Too many plans and schemes. Too many maybes that had turned into nevers. Too many—well, yes, admit it—too many hopes, coming close to dreams, that had turned to ash in his hands.

One too many disillusionments, one more than he could take.

He didn't know which was worse. The rage that pounded at his temples, making it impossible to think straight, or the feeling of having been taken for a fool and used cold-bloodedly.

'Too many people—and all of them we had to smile at,

148

whether we wanted to or not,' Estrella went on, still in that infuriatingly uneven voice.

He couldn't tell what was putting that note into her words. Was it excitement—a sense of triumph at having got exactly what she wanted? Or was it perhaps uncertainty—that she was trying to find out just what he had discussed with her father? Could she really not know?

He doubted it was any real sense of nervousness at the prospect of the future. She had that all worked out—and had from the start.

'I know how that feels.'

'Yes.' Ramón couldn't keep the cynicism out of his voice. Because one of those people she'd had to force herself to smile at had been him. 'I'm sure you do.'

Did she also know how it felt to come to the realisation that you had been played like a fish? Hooked, reeled in, and flung into the net—a net he had only just realised had trapped him?

He'd actually started to think that she was different—that she wasn't as rumour and her reputation had painted her—and he'd been wrong.

Totally bloody wrong.

So wrong that it had shown him at last just what sort of a fool he had been. The sort of blind, besotted, demented fool who forgot all the lessons he had ever learned about looking before he leapt, and jumped right in with both feet, eyes firmly closed.

Damn Alfredo Medrano for not being able to wait to get his hands on the money so that he had moved in for the kill at just the most vulnerable moment. Damn himself for letting down his guard, for making himself vulnerable, just when he should have been gathering his defences up close around him, making sure that nothing got past his guard.

And damn, damn, damn Estrella for having found the chink in what he thought was his impregnable armour.

She must have spotted that weak point right from the start. Seen it and worked on it, playing him like an expert until he had taken the bait, and then she had reeled him in, slowly, oh, so slowly, so that he had never once suspected what was happening to him.

Damn her to hell!

With a furious sigh, he rubbed the back of his hand across his forehead, wishing that he could erase the dark, unwanted thoughts that lingered there, then froze as he felt the soft touch on his other hand, the one that rested on his thigh.

'Don't!'

It was dragged from him as his body responded instantly to just the feel of her fingers on his. He would have thought that the rage that was boiling inside him would have burned away all trace of sensuality, destroying any hint of pleasure at any contact, but instead it was exactly the opposite. Somehow the way he was feeling made him shockingly more sensitive, hunger roaring into existence between one breath and another.

'Don't,' he said again, on a very different note this time, almost pleading so that he winced inwardly to hear it.

'Ramón, what's wrong?'

She actually sounded concerned, so much so that it twisted his gut into knots of disgust and rejection. Perhaps it still suited her to play things that way.

The scent of her perfume was stronger now, coiling round him, making him feel angry and nauseous where only this morning he had loved the subtle mixture of flowers and spices. Now he knew he would hate that smell for ever, always linking it to this moment and the bitter sense of betrayal in his thoughts.

'I knew she'd see sense in the end...'

Alfredo's voice sounded in his thoughts, making his stomach come close to heaving.

'It was a close run thing. But when it came to the prospect of losing everything... She knew I meant it. That if she didn't make a decent marriage for herself she'd get nothing—not a peseta. She soon shaped up after that.'

Estrella had never mentioned the threat to disinherit her. Somehow he'd managed to control his own reactions, refusing to let the old man needle him, to let him see that his words had hit home.

'Well, you got what you wanted out of this,' he'd managed stiffly. 'Your daughter is a married woman now.'

Alfredo had nodded his grey head, his smile one of gloating triumph.

'And she got what she wanted too. No one walks out on Estrella the way you did. I knew she'd make you pay for that. And she has.'

The words struck a sour note in Ramón's thoughts.

'I'm not paying for anything! I chose to marry Estrella.'

'You think you did, but in the end you had no choice. She went after you just the way she went after Perea. "It'll be Ramón Dario, or no one," she said. And now she's got you on a string, dancing to her tune, just like she had that other poor fool.'

'Ramón?'

To his horror, Estrella sounded even closer than before.

His eyes snapped open, clouded grey staring straight into troubled ebony, a faint frown pulling her fine brows together.

You knew that your father planned to disinherit you.

The accusation burned on his tongue so that he almost spat it out, right in her face.

All this talk of freedom, of wanting me, was a lie. In the end all that mattered was the money. You married me, used me to get the money.

If he had known from the start, then it might not have been so bad. If she'd been open, honest, he might have handled it. Might even have been able to go along with it. But she hadn't told him the truth. Not once. Instead she had lied and manipulated him, made him feel sorry for her, then used him as just another conquest, in the same way that she had used Carlos.

'Do you have a headache?'

There it was again, that touch of her fingertips on his skin once more, this time smoothing out the deep crease of a frown between his brows. A crease he didn't even know was there.

She was leaning over him, the warmth of her skin reaching him, the scent of her body tantalising his nostrils. Her mouth was just inches from his own, slightly parted, her white teeth showing in the space between her lips. The smooth, pale lines of her neck in the gathering shadows of the night were a temptation he had to struggle to resist, the need to press his mouth against her, feel her warmth, taste her, almost overwhelming him.

At the base of her throat the sparkling diamond lay against her skin, lifting gently with each indrawn breath, catching the light of the headlights as other vehicles passed them. If he let his gaze drop lower, to the low-cut neckline of the fine black top she wore, he could see the smooth curve where her breasts pushed against the clinging material, the shadowed valley between them…

He had dreamed of putting his head there tonight. Of burying his face between the warm softness of her breasts, pressing his mouth to the satiny flesh, kissing his way…

'No! Yes,' he amended hastily when he saw her faint

recoil and knew that she had taken his protest as denying the headache she had queried.

He was going to have this out with her; he had to. But not now. Not with Paco in the driving seat, a stolid, diplomatically silent presence, but there none the less. He wanted to tear into her, verbally at least, but it would have to wait until they reached the villa and were truly on their own.

'Estrella—leave it,' he muttered. 'I'm tired. It's been a long day.

A long day, and it wasn't going to have the ending he'd anticipated.

Every time he'd looked up and seen Estrella, his thoughts had gone to the time when they would leave the reception. To the moments when, alone at last, they could truly be together. When he could take her in his arms and kiss her until they were both senseless with longing, until their minds were blown, incapable of thought, and the only thing they wanted was to lose themselves in the hungry demands of their flesh.

But that had been when he had thought of her in a very different way. When she had seemed like someone else. Someone he wanted...

'All right!'

She clearly wasn't pleased, her tone and a flash of something in her eyes told him that, but she did as she was asked, moving away, throwing herself back in her seat, folding her arms and sitting stiffly with almost the rest of the back seat separating them.

Immediately, and perversely, he regretted his behaviour. He wanted her close. Wanted to feel her body against his, have his arms around her. Not in the way that he had thought it would happen, of course. He no longer trusted her, and the anger at the way that she had used him still seethed in his soul, filling his mouth with the taste of acid.

But still he wanted her. Fool that he was, all the anger and the distrust and the disillusionment couldn't stop that. He knew what she was on the inside, but it didn't stop him from hankering after the outside. That was still beautiful, still sexy—so desirable.

And she was his wife.

'Come here.'

'What?'

Estrella couldn't believe she had heard right. One moment Ramón had been telling her to go away—to go to hell, his voice and his expression said. She had tried everything she could think of to make him tell her what was wrong, but he had pushed her away, mentally, if not physically. His eyes were cold and distant as Arctic ice floes and nothing seemed to reach him.

Then, just as she had given up, suddenly he had changed his mind.

'Come here,' he'd said, and he'd held up a hand crooking an arrogant finger, summoning her to his side.

She thought of rebelling. Actually considered refusing, but the moment of revolt didn't last long. How could it, when he was her husband and she loved him? Besides, if she was to put into action the plan she had formed to win him over, hold him for ever, then this was the only way she could do it. She had to make him desire her in order to make him want to keep her, and she couldn't do that with the space of the empty seat between them.

'Estrella…'

It was a note of warning, a warning she knew she should heed or risk ruining the night once and for all. So she moved to his side, felt his arms close around her, and melted into the heat and strength of him. And knew in the space of a heartbeat just why she could never really fight this man, never truly rebel against him.

Heat sizzled along her nerves, her blood thundered at her temples and the racing of her heart made it difficult to breathe. Everything tightened, tensed, a restless ache beginning to throb low down, at the most female centre of her body. He hadn't even had to kiss her and she was lost.

But she wanted him to kiss her. And so she lifted her face, with her dark head resting against the equally dark cloth of his elegant jacket, turned her mouth to his...

She didn't have to ask. Didn't have to say a word. He knew what she wanted, and he responded with a speed that made her heart lift, her blood sing. If his kiss was rough rather than gentle, almost cruel instead of enticing, she genuinely didn't mind. This Ramón, this man who was her husband, was someone new, someone dark and disturbing, someone she didn't understand. But she knew one way to reach him. The way she had always reached him.

She was reaching him now, and that was all that mattered. His uncontrolled response, the way he hauled her up close to him, the crush of his mouth on hers, all told her that without any need of words. He used the sway of the car as it rounded the bends in the road, letting it throw her up against him, landing almost in his lap in spite of the restraint of the seat belts.

And all the time he kissed her.

The hard, almost brutal kiss changed abruptly, became deeply sensual, enticing, provoking. It drew her soul out of her body, made her head spin. Strong, urgent hands pushed the sides of her jacket apart, sliding in under the satin lining, smoothing over the clinging material of her top, finding the tiny gap between it and the cream coloured trousers.

The faint burn of his fingertips tracing the exposed line of her skin made her gasp into his mouth and strain closer, the movement opening the gap even wider.

Ramón took advantage of the easier access to her body,

tracing burning, erotic patterns over the exposed flesh, inching higher, higher with every stroke of his hands, so that she writhed in a mixture of delight and impatience.

Ramón's laughter against her mouth was a sound of both triumph and a wordless agreement, his caressing hands trailing still higher, dancing along the swell of the underside of her breasts, skimming the sensitive skin until she moaned aloud in protest.

'Ramón!'

He knew exactly what she meant, what she needed, but he still played his tormenting, tantalising game for a few moments more, dragging it out until she was whimpering in protest. Only then did he slide his knowing fingers round to her narrow back, unclipping her bra with the ease of experience.

The full experience of his touch on her aroused flesh was almost like an explosion in Estrella's mind. She couldn't see, couldn't hear, had lost all awareness of where she was. She could do nothing but give herself up to this man, to the dark sensuality his touch, his kisses woke in her, every part of her being centred on the stinging pleasure of his fingers playing with her breasts, stroking, teasing, tugging at the swollen nipples. Tormenting her with the need for more.

So much so that when one of those wicked hands moved away, slipping lower, she moaned another protest, only to let it subside into a sigh of delight as the warm fingers found a new way to tantalise, sliding into the tight space between her body and the fit of her trousers, cupping her buttocks, stroking her hips.

She was in such a delirium of needy pleasure that she didn't notice that they had stopped, the car drawing to a halt, the driver saying something to Ramón. When he hastily straightened up, pulling away from her, removing his hand, she muttered a petulant protest, catching hold of his jaw as he lifted his head, trying to pull it back down to her.

'Estrella!' Ramón's voice was a blend of exasperated reproach and wicked laughter in the darkness of the now-silent car. 'We're here! We've arrived.'

Then, as she blinked in stunned awakening from the fever that had held her he caught her face in his hands, pressed a swift, hard kiss on her parted lips.

'Just wait, *mi Estrella,* my little sex kitten. Wait. Paco is not staying—he will just unload the cases, and go. I will get rid of him as quickly as I can, I promise you. And then you will be all mine. Be patient—but stay hungry.'

Stay hungry! Estrella reflected dazedly. How could she do anything else when every nerve was screaming with the need for fulfilment he had woken in it, when she couldn't think, couldn't speak, could only feel?

Somehow she staggered out of the car, kept upright only by the muscular arm that Ramón clamped around her waist, holding her tight against the strong support of his body. He didn't let go for a moment and Estrella could only be grateful for his help, knowing that her blurred eyesight, the unsteady feeling in her legs, would soon have resulted in her collapsing in a pitiable heap on the floor if he were ever to loosen his grip. But at the same time as that powerful support was a source of comfort, it also caused her a new wave of agony as it intensified and added to the explosive hunger deep inside, making her want him more than ever before.

She barely noticed how Ramón supervised the offloading of their bags, was only vaguely aware of his thanks to Paco, the inordinately generous tip he gave the chauffeur to speed him on his way. She wouldn't have known if it was night or day, when Ramón kicked the door shut and turned to her, only that now, at last, they were alone.

'Alone…'

It was the only word she'd attempted for a while and she was stunned to find that she could actually manage it, even if her voice did sound so raw and croaky that it seemed to come from a very sore throat indeed.

'Alone,' Ramón echoed. 'And still hungry.'

CHAPTER THIRTEEN

STILL hungry…

If it had been a question, not a statement, Ramón didn't wait around for an answer. He didn't even bother to put the lights on, but swung Estrella up into his arms and headed for the stairs, finding his way in the darkness with the ease of a cat.

The bedroom was full of moonlight, bright enough to see by. Not that Ramón gave her any chance to look round. Even as he let her slide to the ground his hands were busy peeling off the jacket, ripping away the insubstantial clinging top. Her bra was still unfastened after his attentions earlier and that too was flung away, tossed into some dark corner of the room.

The next stage took a little longer. Not because Ramón fumbled or hesitated, but because he set himself to kiss his way over her body, starting at the top of her head, and moving down, down…

Estrella felt the warmth of his mouth on her face, on her nose, briefly on her lips, before it continued on its sensual journey, devoting such time and attention to her shoulders, her breasts, the softness of her stomach where his tongue traced the indentation of her navel, that by the time he reached the slight barrier of her trousers she was already a trembling wreck, longing to sink to her knees on the floor.

But, 'No,' Ramón muttered as her nerveless body started to sag. He pushed her upright again, warning her with a flash of molten silver eyes to stay where she was while his hands dispensed with the remaining items of her clothing, sliding them down onto the floor at her feet.

Still his kisses went on, lower, and lower, through the curls at the joining of her thighs, along the smooth inner skin of her legs. But when he kissed her intimately she couldn't stop herself.

'Ramón!' she sighed protestingly, reaching down to clutch at his wide shoulders, needing something to support her. 'Ramón, please. I want you—I need you.'

He needed no further encouraging. He didn't even get up off his knees, but tumbled her backwards onto the big cushiony bed. And he came with her, his long body covering hers, his kisses driving her to distraction so that she clutched at him, tugging his clothes from him, fumbling with the belt at his waist, muttering aloud in her impatience and need.

'Steady!' Ramón laughed, but steady was the last thing she felt.

With a small choking cry in her throat she freed him, reaching for the hot hardness of him, only to be thwarted when he caught her wanton hands in one of his.

'No!' he muttered. 'That won't do. Not now...'

Lifting her hands above her head and pinioning them there on the pillows, he was already sliding between her thighs, using the pressure and strength of one hard, hairroughened leg to part hers. In the space of a couple of heartbeats from the moment when she had fallen backwards onto the bed, he was lying between her thighs, the force of his erection already pushing at the core of her femininity.

There was a wild streak of colour on his broad cheekbones, and the eyes that burned down into her had a febrile glitter that spoke of just how close to the edge he was himself.

'What I want is this...'

On the last word he pushed himself into her, finding her

already so aroused and hungry for him that the single powerful thrust almost pushed her over the edge in a moment.

But he wasn't prepared to let her climax quite that fast. Instantly he stilled, subjecting her already-throbbing body to yet more kisses, more caresses, finding every waiting, nerve, greedy for sensation, every pleasure spot she had ever known, and some she hadn't even been aware existed. Eyes closed, Estrella flung her head back on the downy pillows, thrashing from side to side, wondering how much more she could endure, wanting it to go on and on—and yet also desperate to know that vital soaring moment of release before she exploded.

'Oh, Ramón—please…'

It was all she could manage. Every fuse in her mind had blown, her eyes were blind, her ears deaf. She was locked into the sensations that drove her so close to distraction—and never quite there.

'Please, please, please, please!'

In the end she was reduced to begging, knowing she could take no more. And at last he started to move, her own name suddenly a muttered litany on his lips, his voice husky and raw with loss of restraint, his breath warm and ragged on her face.

It seemed that he had been barely holding himself in check too, his stillness the only thing that had kept him from losing control. Because it was only a second or two before his long body clenched, his jaw tightening on a muttered curse.

The next moment any hold they had on actuality slipped totally away. There was no sight, no sound, nothing in the world but each other and the wild sensations they were creating together. Another choking cry escaped her, only to be crushed back down her throat by the force of his lips. And in the same instant the white hot explosion of delight overpowered her, throwing her out of reality and into a world of stars and meteors and blinding, brilliant light.

It was a long, long time before Estrella's thought processes started to work again. Slowly her head stopped spinning, her breathing slowed, her heart rate settled down to a normal patter once more. But she felt worn out, exhausted by the long, emotional day, drifting in and out of sleep several times before she finally stirred, groaned, blinked her eyes, stretched…

And froze as something communicated itself to her through the silence in the room.

It was not the comfortable silence she had expected. Not the close, comfortable silence of two people who had just made wild passionate love, exhausting themselves so that they fell asleep in each other's arms.

She was not in Ramón's arms. In fact, Ramón was…

Where was Ramón?

Forcing her eyes open, she struggled up to a half-sitting position, leaning on one elbow, staring round, to see Ramón sitting on the edge of the bed.

'What are you doing?'

Without a word needing to be spoken, she felt every sense sounding a fearful alarm, warning her of danger. She was still totally naked, though someone—Ramón, obviously— had pulled a sheet over her as she slept. But he was fully dressed in the black trousers and white shirt she had tugged off him such a short time before. And he was watching her through disturbingly cold, assessing eyes.

'What—what are you doing?'

'Waiting for you to wake up.' The words were as cold as his icy glare, chilling her right through to her heart in the time it took to draw in a single, uneven breath.

'Why? Has something happened? Is something wrong?'

His smile froze her blood, and a cold, cruel hand gripped the nerves in her stomach and twisted hard.

'Of course not—everything's gone exactly as you expected it.'

'As I...? I don't know what you mean.'

She actually looked bemused, Ramón reflected cynically, seeing the frown that drew her brows together, the dazed expression in her eyes. She actually looked as if she didn't know what he meant. He wanted to laugh out loud at the fact that she was even trying to act a part he knew she wasn't qualified for. But at the same time, deep down and unwanted in his heart was the reluctant, uncomfortable thought that maybe, just maybe she didn't know what he was talking about.

No, that couldn't be... She had to know.

'You got just what you wanted.'

'Oh—yes.' Smiling, she stretched luxuriously. 'Yes, I did.'

Her smile was like a stiletto blade sliding into his heart, creating a wound that, while agonising, was not yet fatal— not yet. Was he fool enough to still want to cling on to the possibility that she might not have used him as badly as he had thought?

'And you.'

Suddenly she sat upright, pulling the sheet with her.

'You did get what you wanted, didn't you? This isn't because my father went back on the deal?'

He shook his dark head, but the gesture did nothing to ease the hard, tense set of his handsome features. They remained as cold and distant as ever.

'Oh, no—your *papá* was only too keen to sign on the dotted line.'

Of course he was. Ramón wanted to shake his head again, but this time in despair at himself. He should have learned from old Alfredo—like father, like daughter should have been his watchword. But instead he'd let other, weaker feelings drive him.

'So what are you in such a bad mood about?'

'I've been thinking about our marriage...'

And he hadn't come to any damn conclusions. Earlier he had told himself that this changed nothing. That he had known she wasn't marrying him for love or anything like, so why should the realisation that she had lied about why she was not marrying for love change anything?

'So have I.'

Sliding towards him on the mattress, she put a hand on his arm, stroked the skin exposed where he had pushed up the sleeves of his shirt.

'It was the first thing in my mind when I woke up.'

It was all he could do not to respond. He wanted to respond, dammit; it was hell not responding. Her skin was still pink from the heat of their passion, her eyes heavy, their lids slightly drooping from tiredness, drowsy from sleep. The ridiculously ornate hair style had pulled loose in places in the fury of their lovemaking so that long black strands of it hung, tangled and loose around her face.

His fingers itched to reach up and smooth them back, tuck them behind her ears, but he knew that if he so much as touched her he would never be able to hold back again.

So he forced himself to sit there, cold and stiff as a marble statue, his eyes blanked off, jaw set.

'Oh, Ramón, that can't be what's upset you...'

Moving closer, she rested her head against his shoulder, letting go of the sheet so that it began to slither slowly and seductively down her body.

He knew damn well what was happening. She wanted to distract him, and she was using seduction to do so. But he didn't want to be distracted. Earlier, in the car, he had told himself that it didn't matter. That he had married her because she wanted him and he wanted her—and he still wanted her, more than ever.

It could still work, he'd resolved, he could settle for that. He had settled for that—just now—here on this bed.

And it hadn't been enough. Not enough to satisfy him—not really. Not enough to wipe from his mind the way that she'd lied to him, used him.

Not enough.

'We both know that we can make this marriage work.'

She'd lowered her voice to a husky whisper. One that coiled round his nerves, tormented his senses, made the burn of need clutch at him savagely and cruelly—cruelly because he knew he had to fight it. Sex was no answer, even if Estrella believed it was.

Sex would fade—it might even die completely. And what would they be left with then? What would she want when the fun of having him in her power had waned and she looked around for newer toys to play with? Hell, even his mother had actually never schemed to get Juan Alcolar into her bed. She had fallen in love with him totally unexpectedly.

'We went into it with our eyes open. We both knew what we wanted—and we got it.'

'But you got so much more than you claimed you wanted.'

That stopped her dead, stilling her so suddenly that she actually left her mouth hanging part way open in stunned amazement. Her black eyes looked as dazed as if someone had slapped her hard in the face and there was a wary expression in them as she turned them on his face.

'More than—more than... Oh, yes.'

She laughed.

She actually, damn well laughed. Starting as a slightly

nervous giggle, moving into something disturbingly high-pitched and almost out of control, it grated on his raw nerves, notched the tension up several more degrees.

And brought the rage rushing back into his mind.

'Yes, I got so much more than I ever expected. But I never thought you'd realise that.'

'Never thought!'

It was a roar of blind fury. Fury and pain in a deadly combination, so that his ability to think straight was blasted, the red haze of wrath flooding his mind until he couldn't see, could only feel.

He couldn't stand to be near her any longer. Couldn't sit here while she cuddled up to him, resting her head on his shoulder, clearly thinking that all she had to do was to kiss him again, to let that damn sheet slip a little lower...

No! Wrenching himself away from her so savagely that she lost her balance and went sprawling on the bed, he flung himself to his feet in a movement that took him halfway across the room, whirling to face her, glare at her, though the mist before his eyes meant that he couldn't actually see the details of her lying, conniving face.

'So you're admitting to it! Telling me it's true?'

'Yes—I think...'

Her voice was only faint through the monstrous buzzing in his ears, and suddenly she stopped, going very still and white.

'H-how did you know?'

'Your father, of course!' Ramón flung at her, biting off the words in his anger. 'You surely didn't think he wouldn't tell me—and enjoy doing it?'

'My—father...? Ramón, what are we talking about here?'

'Oh, don't give me that!' he exploded. 'Don't try to go back on it now, Doña Estrella, not when you've already admitted that it was true. You and your father got exactly what you planned for. You got your marriage—even if only to the tenth on the list—and the inheritance that depended on it. You even got the unexpected bonus of a husband you wanted in your bed. Was that what was wrong with the others, Estrella—that you weren't hot for them?'

She didn't try to answer, and even if she had he wouldn't have listened. Instead he rushed on, driven only by fury.

'Your father got the return to respectability he wanted—the prospect of a grandchild to inherit—he got some mug to buy his company. And I—I got stitched up completely!'

'No!' Estrella tried to put in, but he refused to hear her.

'Yes, damn you, yes! But no more, *querida!* No more—do you hear me? No more! I've had enough—all I can take! You got your marriage, so I hope it was worth it. And you had better hope that what we did tonight, in that bed, had the result your *papá* wanted too. If you really dreamed of presenting him with a grandson for the title and the inheritance, then you'd better start praying that you're already pregnant. Because if you're not, then I swear to God that I'll never damn well touch you again.'

'Ramón—' Estrella began, but he couldn't bear to hear her.

He couldn't stand to be in the room with her any longer. If he did, he knew that he would do something that he would regret. He would either kiss her or kill her, and right now he didn't know if the temptation to one was stronger than the other.

And both of them would have an appalling, disastrous effect.

So, not wanting to face the consequences if he stayed, he turned on his heel and marched out of the room, down the stairs and across the hall to the front door. Barely even breaking his stride, he yanked it open so roughly that it slammed against the wall with a heavy thud. A moment later he was through the doorway and out in the cool of the night air.

He kept on walking, not knowing where he was going, not caring, wanting only to put as much distance between himself and his brand-new wife as he possibly could.

CHAPTER FOURTEEN

ESTRELLA couldn't believe that she had actually fallen asleep.

She hadn't meant to. She certainly had never wanted to. She had planned to stay wide awake, just listening and waiting for Ramón to come back.

He had to come back, she told herself. However angry he was—and he had been enraged—he couldn't just walk out of the house, out of her life and disappear. Or could he?

He had been furious enough to do it. So furious that it seemed to have put wings on his feet and although she had flung herself off the bed and after him as soon as she'd been able to think clearly enough—which had taken the space of a few moments—she hadn't been able to catch him. He had been out of the house before she'd even reached the stairs, the slam of the door behind him echoing round the silent hallway.

So she'd dashed back to the room, pulling on clothes, stuffing her feet into her shoes, as fast as she could, but knowing all the time in the depths of her desolated heart, that she had no hope at all of finding where he'd gone, or being able to follow after him.

Which of course had proved to be the case. There had been no sign of him in the courtyard outside the villa, no sight of his tall, strong figure on the road where the moonlight beat down with cold indifference, making it almost as bright as day so that there had been little room for doubt.

She had trailed back inside the house, feeling so low that she could hardly pick up her feet to move, and had forced herself upstairs with a struggle. She would sit here and wait for him, she had told herself, settling on the bed and propping herself up on the pillows. He had to come back at some point.

And while she waited she would go back over that appalling row they had had before he had walked out, and try and work out just what had happened. Where it had all gone wrong.

Because something had gone terribly wrong. And it hadn't been because of what she had believed.

'But you got so much more than you claimed you wanted,' Ramón had flung at her and in the heat of the moment, overwrought, overtired, and totally bewildered by the sudden change that had come over him, she had believed that he had found her out. Thinking that he had meant that he knew she had fallen in love with him, she had seen no other way to answer him but to tell him the truth.

She had even laughed. Nervous and uncontrollable, she had felt the giggle rise up inside her and escape as almost a sound of relief. Yes, she had wanted to say, I've fallen in love with you. I'm sorry if it's not what you want, but it's come as as much of a shock to me as it obviously is to you. But surely this doesn't have to spoil anything?

But he hadn't given her a chance, and she had been horrified by the violence of his reaction, the way he had turned on her, the accusations he had thrown at her before he had stormed out.

You and your father got exactly what you planned for.

And I—I got stitched up completely!

She had got what she wanted? And what about that damn TV company?

Too miserable to scream, too strung up to cry, Estrella had only been able to sit there, counting the minutes, jumping at every strange and inexplicable sound, waiting for

Ramón—and praying that he would come back, even if it was only to collect his belongings.

At some point she had fallen asleep without knowing it. All that she did know was that she had closed her eyes for a moment and when she had opened them again something about a change in the light warned her that more of the night had passed since she had last looked at the window. A swift glance at a clock told her that it was four a.m. The lowest, darkest hour of the night.

The darkest hour is just before dawn. The saying ran inside her head, making her feel more miserable rather than better. An emotional dawn could only come if Ramón had returned so that they could have a chance to talk, to try and sort things out.

But the house was as still and silent as ever before.

And she felt miserable as sin.

Her clothes were crumpled and grubby from having been slept in. The elaborate hairstyle was little more than a bird's nest—and a badly built bird's nest at that—she had a pounding stress headache and was parched, desperate for something to drink.

A cup of coffee might help the physical symptoms, she told herself. It was hours since they had left the wedding reception, and the after effects of a little too much champagne, little solid food, and a night of emotional storms had taken its toll on her. After that, she might be able to think straight enough to come up with some plan of action.

But first she had to find the kitchen.

She couldn't even find the light switches in the unknown rooms, and had to find her way downstairs by groping along the wall in the darkness, going down the steps one at a time and as carefully as possible. The hall and the living room were equally dark, their cases—hers and Ramón's—standing in a pool of moonlight where they had dumped them hours before.

Now which way would she turn to find the kitchen?

'There's a light switch just to your right...'

A voice came out of the darkness, making her start and scream faintly in shock.

'Don't panic,' Ramón said quietly. 'It's only me. About shoulder height.'

After a couple of seconds' clumsy searching, she found it, clicked it on, flooding the room with light so that she blinked hard in the sudden brightness.

Ramón sat in one of the big black armchairs at the far side of the room, beside the wide, empty fireplace. He looked dreadful, Estrella had to admit. His hair was desperately tousled, blown everywhere by the wind that she now realised she could hear outside, there were heavy shadows under the once brilliant eyes, which were now dull and lacklustre, and the heavy growth of beard that had darkened his cheeks and jaw with stubble made him look like some disreputable tramp.

'How did you get in?'

Inane as it was, it was all she could manage.

'I have a key.' His voice was low and flat, as emotionless as his face.

'I didn't hear you.'

'Probably because I didn't want to wake you.'

Now how did she interpret that? Had he not wanted to wake her out of consideration for her, or because he just hadn't wanted to talk to her? After all, he had left her with the impression that if he never saw her again it would be too soon.

'How long have you been here?'

Shadowed grey eyes glanced at the clock, then back at her face.

'An hour or so. Perhaps ninety minutes.'

'And you've been sitting all that time in the dark?'

Ramón nodded sombrely.

'I had a lot of thinking to do.'

'Oh.'

It was all she could manage. She didn't dare to ask him what he had been thinking about—she suspected that she already knew. And she wasn't really sure whether she wanted to know what conclusions he had come to. He would probably tell her soon enough.

So she took refuge in more inanities, and the simple practical reasons why she had come downstairs in the first place.

'I—I was going to make a drink. Would you like one?'

The words were hardly out of her mouth when he had pushed himself to his feet in one lithe, supple movement, his gaze going towards a door on the far side of the room.

'I'll do it. You sit down.'

'But I—' Estrella tried to protest, only to break off when he raised a hand to silence her.

'It's easier if I do it. I know where everything is. Coffee or something stronger?'

'Coffee, please.'

Anything alcoholic would just finish her off. She was so worn out, in spite of her catnap, that it would go straight to her head and leave her incapable of talking any sense.

Not that she felt she could string more than three coherent words together, she admitted as he headed for what she presumed was the kitchen. Shock had turned her brain to mush, incapable of functioning.

Ramón had been here for the past hour—perhaps more—and he hadn't woken her. Had he even come upstairs to see if she was all right? The words so near and yet so far away wouldn't stop repeating in her head.

'What—what were you thinking about?'

The question came so quietly, so hesitantly, that she was sure he hadn't heard her until he paused briefly in the doorway and looked back at her.

'When I've made the coffee,' he said. 'We'll talk then.'

Estrella couldn't work out his mood from his tone, and those eyes were giving nothing away. But at least he had said that they would talk. For now, she would have to be content with that. To insist on anything more would probably alienate him, drive him away again, and she didn't want to risk that. And so she made herself sit down in one of the chairs and prepared to wait.

What were you thinking about? So how did he answer that? Ramón asked himself, his hands, working purely on autopilot, busy filling a kettle, getting coffee, milk, cups.

What had he been thinking of?

Estrella, of course.

Estrella and nothing but Estrella. Estrella and their relationship. Whether they had a relationship. Whether he wanted a relationship. And if he did, just where did they go from here?

Always assuming that she wanted to go anywhere. Which was something he had no idea about.

There was a hell of a lot he had no idea about. And thinking hadn't done very much to help.

Making the coffee didn't take long enough. Far too soon the small task was done and he had to take the drinks back into the other room where Estrella was sitting, dwarfed by the oversized black velvet-covered chair.

'Here…'

He dumped the coffee-cup on a table near her, then took his own to the chair opposite, deciding at the last minute that he felt too restless, too much on pins to sit down, and opting for leaning against the wall instead, watching her.

He already knew she was dressed. When he had come

back to the dark, silent house after several hours of walking and walking in a vain attempt to clear his head, he had crept up to the bedroom to check on her. She had fallen asleep on the bed, having pulled on her going-away outfit—well, the cream-coloured trousers and jacket, at least. The black camisole top had been ripped beyond repair in the heat of their passion. The torn remnants of it still lay on the floor upstairs, at the foot of the bed.

Ramón wished devoutly that it had been fit to wear. At least then she wouldn't look so sexily enticing as she did now, with the jacket buttoned over her bare skin, the soft curves of the tops of her breasts exposed to view. It was too distracting this way, and he didn't want to be distracted. He was already far too vulnerable where she was concerned.

The thought made him start uncomfortably, slopping coffee over into his saucer.

Vulnerable. Yes, that was what he had been thinking about all this time, alone in the dark. He had been thinking about the way he felt, and why that made him so damnably vulnerable to everything about this woman.

'So what did you want to talk about?'

'I don't think this marriage has any future,' he said bluntly. 'It isn't going to work out.'

'But why not? What's changed?'

'What's changed? Well, try the fact that I married you to help you. You said you needed rescuing from your father's matchmaking schemes. You needed to escape.'

'And I did.'

Estrella's fingers were clamped so tight on the handle of her coffee-cup that her knuckles showed white and she looked even paler than ever before.

'You know I did—you saw...'

'I saw what you wanted me to see,' Ramón put in scathingly. 'And then only part of it. I saw the poor-little-rich-girl mask you put on—the ''I just have to escape—I don't care how I do it'' act.'

'It wasn't an act!'

'No?'

He gave up all pretence at drinking a coffee he'd never wanted in the first place and deposited the cup on the wooden mantelpiece over the fire.

'No! I swear it! You know what my life was like!'

'I know what you said it was like. For all I know you could have made half of it up. And your father—'

'You don't believe that my father was as bad as I say? That my life wasn't as miserable as I claim? Have you forgotten so quickly? You were there when the t-toad—when Esteban Ramirez—'

'Oh, I saw him!' Ramón cut in. 'And I believed you then. But what I didn't know was that you'd already decided who you wanted in your bed. Just as you'd once decided you wanted Perea.'

It came so unexpectedly and with such a stunning force that Estrella's head actually went back with the shock of it. Numbed, shaking, she stared at him in horror.

'Is that what my father…? Is that what you really believe? You think I—'

Looking round the room, she spotted where her small patent leather handbag had been discarded on the dresser on their arrival. Snatching it up, she tossed it at Ramón, careless of whether he caught it or not.

'Look in there. Go on—open it—take a look.'

Totally bemused, he did as she asked. Inside the bag, along with a few feminine bits and pieces, was a folded white envelope, and inside that was an official-looking document. Signed and stamped and dated.

A wedding certificate.

'What the—'

For a moment Ramón thought it was their marriage certificate, but then he looked again. The print seemed to swim in front of his eyes as he saw the names, the signatures.

Estrella Medrano.

Carlos Perea.

'Estrella, what is this?'

'Can't you see?' Her tone was terribly bitter. 'Can't you read? What do you think it is?'

'It's a marriage certificate.'

He still couldn't believe what he was saying.

'You and Carlos—but—we…'

'Oh, don't worry.'

Estrella too gave up on any pretence that she was drinking her coffee.

'Don't panic. It's not that our marriage is bigamous. It was mine to Carlos that was! Not that he told me, of course. Otherwise, I'd never have been fool enough to marry him.'

'He— You *married* him.'

'How do you think he persuaded me to go with him?'

The bitter edge to her words was fraying. Her voice was starting to quaver and there was a suspicious brightness in her eyes. Ramón felt as if he had been thumped hard in the face.

'You really didn't know he was married?'

'He swore he wasn't!'

'But how could you not know?'

'Carlos had lived in the area before but he'd moved away. I was away too—at school—and then at college. I didn't know what had happened to him in the meantime. All I knew was that he was back. His wife and children were still in their old home, in another town—her mother was ill and she was staying to look after her. I suppose no one ever said anything because they all knew—and they just assumed I did.'

She needed to draw a steadying breath before she could go on and it was that, and the way that her hands were clenched tight at her sides, that added conviction to the hurt in her voice, twisting mercilessly at his already painful conscience.

'He made me promise to keep our meetings secret—said my father would never approve. Which, of course, he wouldn't have done. I know now that he only wanted to sleep with me—but he said—he knew I was too scared—and so he said he wanted to marry me.'

'And that's why you went away with him?' Ramón's voice was raw with the shock of what she was telling him. The realisation that he had been so terribly wrong about her—that everyone had. 'When did you find out the truth?'

Estrella's dark eyes clouded with a recollection of the misery she had endured on that dreadful day.

'When his wife rang the hotel to tell him that—that their little girl was ill and she needed him.'

Ramón's response was short, succinct and extremely violent.

'And you answered the phone?'

'Yes...'

'Oh, Estrella.'

He could only shake his dark head in disbelief at the other man's monstrous behaviour.

'But—you—why didn't you tell anyone?'

Her eyes dropped to stare at the floor and her bare foot moved restlessly, tracing the pattern on the carpet.

'What good would it have done? Carlos was killed in a road accident a week after I found out the truth. His family—his wife and children—were already suffering enough. I couldn't add to it by—by telling them.'

'So you took all the blame.'

Estrella managed a careless shrug.

'I could cope—I never thought it would go on for so long. And I was used to being a disappointment to my father. I always had been, from the moment I was born. I was the wrong sex, you see. My father only has time for sons, and unfortunately he had none of those. I was my parents' last chance. My father was over fifty when I was born and my mother couldn't have any more children. What he wanted was a male heir to take over the estate. To marry a suitably quiet, well-behaved, well-connected young woman who would give him more boys—grandsons to carry on the Medrano line. What he got…'

She paused, looked down at herself briefly, cynically, then swept her hands in a revealing gesture along the length of her slender body.

'Me,' she stated flatly. 'He got me and he's never really forgiven me or my mother ever since.'

'I don't see how anyone could possibly be disappointed in you,' Ramón said, knowing that he meant it. 'I knew your father was a mean-minded fool—but this proves it. And I'm another one for ever believing a thing he said.'

That brought her head up, a faint, weak smile on her pale face.

'I—I did tell him that the only one of his suitors I would ever consider would be you.'

'And the rest of it? Were you ever going to tell me that?'

'Why do you think that envelope was in my bag? Because I just happen to carry with me the certificate from my first, illegal and totally unreal marriage? I was going to show it to you! To tell you the truth—tell you everything. I was going to do it last night—but you—but we…'

She choked off the words, but the way her eyes went to the open door, looking at the stairs beyond, told their own story.

'I'm sorry.'

It was all he could say. He couldn't think of anything else, anything to show that he sympathised—that he understood—that he detested the way the other man had deceived her.

'And your father blamed you for this?'

Her mouth twisted into a bitter line.

'You know my father—men are always saints, until they're led astray by wicked, wanton women. So I had to have been the sinner—and Carlos was the sinned against.'

'I'd like to kill the bastard.'

Her second smile was tiny, faint and wan but it was there. A spark of the old Estrella he had known, and it tore at his heart because of that.

'I don't think that would do much good now. But—but thank you all the…'

Her voice broke on a little hiccupping sob, and before Ramón knew that he had moved he was there, beside her, coming down on his knees to put his arms around her, hold her tight.

'I am sorry,' he said hoarsely. 'I'm so sorry. I should have known…'

Estrella buried her head in his shoulder for a moment and he felt the dampness of tears on his shirt. All he could do was stroke her back, her hair…

She wished she could stay here like this, Estrella told herself. Wished she could just stay here in his arms, and never, ever have to lift her head again. Being here felt so right, so safe, so secure—but it couldn't last for ever. And it wouldn't solve whatever it was that had angered Ramón so much that he had wanted to leave her.

At last the sobs subsided and she sniffed inelegantly, swiping at her eyes with the back of her hand as she lifted her head. Dark, tear-filled eyes looked deep into watchful

silvery grey, and she knew the truth of what she had suspected. That this wasn't the real root of the problem.

'But—but that wasn't it, was it?' she managed. 'That
wasn't what made you so angry. There's something else.'

He actually looked awkward and a touch embarrassed,
getting up from his knees to sit on the arm of the chair
beside her.

'It can wait.'

'No, it can't! I won't let you! If you're going to accuse
me of lies and of—of stitching you up, then you can at least
have the decency to say on what evidence. Who told you?'

Ramón sighed and pushed both hands through his hair.

'Your father.'

'My father? What did he say? What has he told you? And
why do you believe him when you know that he'll do anything—say anything…?'

'So it isn't true that he said he'd disown you if you didn't
marry.'

'Oh.'

It was all that she could say, her mind too numb with
shock to let her manage anything else. And what else could
she say? There was no way she could deny it; her silence
made that plain. Ramón pounced on that like a tiger
springing on its prey.

'It is true, isn't it? He told you you'd have no money—
nothing—unless you married.'

'Yes.'

'What?'

Ramón leaned forward, his stunning face darkly intent.

'What was that? I didn't hear you.'

'I said yes—yes—yes—yes! My father said he'd cut me
off without a penny—that he'd throw me out on the streets.
Do you believe that? Is that what you wanted to know? Are
you happy now?'

'No,' Ramón said, getting up from his seat and prowling round the chair. 'No.'

'No what? No, you don't believe or—'

'No, it doesn't make me damn well happy! It's the last thing I wanted to hear.'

Strangely, she believed him. But at the back of her mind there was a nasty, sneaking suspicion. One that threatened her composure even more strongly than anything else that had happened.

'You think that's why I married you, don't you? That's it! You think I only did it for the money.'

He didn't need to answer; she could read it in his face. The anger, the defiance, a trace of guilt—it was all there. She could tell the truth—prove him wrong, but right now she was just too angry for that.

'You think— How dare you? How the bloody hell dare you?'

'You've admitted—'

'I've admitted nothing. I simply told you that, yes, my father threatened to disinherit me. And you have the nerve to come all moral and holier than thou over that! You— who only married me for the damn TV company!'

'No!'

'Yes! Oh, come on, Ramón!' she mocked. 'Don't try and wriggle out of it now! You haven't got a leg to stand on. Remember, you were the one who told me that my father offered you the deal—that he said you could have it for half what it was worth. And you signed the deal with him to-day—yesterday,' she amended hastily. 'You couldn't even wait! He signed over the company to you on—on our wedding day. Didn't he?'

'Yes.' It was harsh, rough, husky.

'Then—'

'But not for half the price. He wanted to give it to me as a wedding present.'

'Oh, bully for you,' Estrella scorned, the pain eating at her like acid. 'Then you got an even better deal than you thought. Not even half price.'

'No—because I didn't pay—'

'You didn't pay anything. You got it for free.'

'Estrella!'

It was a lion's roar, loud and savage and demanding of respect and it shut her up at once, made her unable to go on.

'I not only didn't get it for free—I paid the whole damn price. The original full asking price. Every peseta he wanted. And I would have paid more if I'd had to.'

That had her mouth opening and closing, trying to say something, but no sound would come out.

'But—' she croaked. 'But—but why?'

'Isn't it obvious?'

'Not to me. Not at all. Why would anyone—especially you—want to pay the full price for something they'd been offered at fifty per cent off—and then been promised as a gift?'

His smile was wry, self-mocking and slightly crooked and the self-deprecation was mirrored in his eyes as he looked into hers and took a deep, deep breath.

'Because I love you.'

And then, when she couldn't find anything to say, but could only stare at him in blank, unbelieving confusion, he shrugged his shoulders and this time he laughed, but in exactly the same self-mocking way.

'Because I love you.'

It was about time he said it, Ramón acknowledged. It was the only answer, the only explanation for the way he'd been feeling. It was just that he had been trying not to admit it, not even to himself.

But even as he'd been walking away from her, he'd known the truth. Why else could the thought that he'd been used, that she'd lied to him, hurt so much, enrage so much? And then, when he'd known he'd had no alternative but to turn round and come back here, he'd also faced the fact that he had no alternative but to admit to what he felt. It was either that or lose her, and he couldn't live with losing her.

'You...'

Estrella was still struggling with his declaration.

'But—but you said that our marriage didn't have a future.'

Once more Ramón pushed both hands through his hair, turning its smooth sleekness into impossible disorder.

'I didn't think it had. Didn't think it would work with just one of us loving the other.'

'But you'd already refused my father's offer.'

'Yeah...'

Once more he was prowling round the room, restless as a trapped tiger.

'It was the only thing I could do—I didn't want you to think I'd only married you to get my hands on the company.'

'But I was the one who suggested it as a basis for our marriage.'

Ramón swung round to face her, knowing there was nothing he could say but the truth.

'And I was the one who couldn't go through with it. Even though then I still hadn't admitted to myself that what I was feeling was love, I just knew I couldn't have our marriage start out in that way. I'd wanted the company, yes, but I wanted you so much more—and I wanted you without any ties and conditions or financial rewards.'

Suddenly, unexpectedly, Estrella moved forward to catch hold of his arm, keep him still, so that he had to look at her, looking down into the burning darkness of her eyes.

'And that was when my father told you that he'd threatened to disinherit me, wasn't it?'

'Yes. Yes, it was.'

'But he didn't make that threat until after I'd asked you to marry me. That day at the castle—when you came to—to propose—when the Toad was there—that was when he gave me the ultimatum. To marry or lose my inheritance.'

Her eyes pleaded with him to believe her. He wanted to believe her. And then suddenly he remembered a story his brother Alex had told him about his new wife Louise and how, at one point, Alex too had been sure that she only wanted him for his money.

'So how did she convince you you'd got it wrong?' he'd asked and Alex had blushed—Alex had actually blushed and said that that was between him and Louise.

'But it wasn't what she did, it was that I knew,' he'd added. 'Suddenly, I just knew that she wouldn't have done it. And no matter what she'd said or done after that, I knew that she just wasn't capable of using me that way.'

'Ramón, please believe me…' Estrella said now, and in that moment Ramón knew that his brother was right. He didn't need any further evidence. He didn't need proof. He just knew.

'I do,' he said, knowing that he meant it. 'I do believe you.'

Estrella drew in a deep breath and let it out again slowly, her heart dancing for joy at what she had just heard. He believed her and he loved her. What more could she ask for?

So now of course it was her turn. And she had to be

quick. She had kept him waiting quite long enough. She had to put him out of his misery fast!

'Ramón—you know how you said that you don't think our marriage would work with just one of us loving the other…?'

The look in his eyes tore at her heart and tears blurred her vision.

'I don't think I could bear it.'

'Don't think you could bear it! Oh, Ramón…'

Moving her hands from his arms, she folded them around his fingers, holding tight.

'Neither do I. So what if it was both of us?'

With her eyes fixed on his, she saw Ramón's momentary confusion, then the sudden look of hope that came with his realisation of what she meant.

'Are you…?'

'Yes,' she told him. 'Yes, I am—I'm telling you that I love you too. I love you with everything that's in my heart and my mind and my soul. That the real reason why I asked you to marry me was because I was falling in love with you and I couldn't stop myself. I'm telling you that you were never number ten on my list—you were always and only my number one. And I'm telling you that I want this to be a proper marriage—a marriage of love and sharing for the rest of our lives. Like you, I couldn't bear anything else.'

She read his answer in his face before he moved to gather her into his arms.

'You won't have to,' he assured her, his voice deep and sincere. 'Our real marriage starts here, with me knowing that you love me and you knowing that I adore you—can't live without you. And to prove it…'

Taking her hand, he drew her out through the huge plate-glass patio doors that led onto the big, paved terrace outside the house. Beyond the balcony, the sun was just beginning to rise, gilding the sky with its fire.

There he repeated and renewed the wedding vows he had made to her the day before, and Estrella repeated hers to him as the dawn broke on the start of a new day, and the start of their loving life together.

Introducing a brand-new miniseries

For *Love* or **MONEY**

This is romance on the red carpet...

For Love or Money is the ultimate reading experience
for the reader who has a taste for tales of wealth and
celebrity and the accompanying gossip and scandal!

Look out for the special covers
and
these upcoming titles:

Coming in November:

SALE OR RETURN BRIDE
by Sarah Morgan

#2500

Coming in December:

TAKEN BY THE HIGHEST BIDDER
by Jane Porter

#2508

Harlequin Presents®
The ultimate emotional experience!

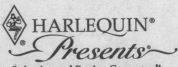

HARLEQUIN®
Presents

Seduction and Passion Guaranteed!

www.eHarlequin.com

HPSORB